Light in the Dark

Light in the Dark

an anthology

Edited by Gill James

Bridge House

British Library Cataloguing in Publication Data

A Record of this Publication is available from the British Library

ISBN 978-1-907335-37-2

This edition published 2014 by Bridge House Publishing Manchester, England

All Bridge House books are published on paper derived from sustainable resources.

Contents

Introduction

Why *Light in the Dark?* Perhaps because for this anthology we asked for thought-provoking stories and many of the ones we liked were leaning towards the darker side. Yet not a single one is completely dark, They all lean towards the light and there is some hope: the faint light of a candle growing in the dark.

In any case the collection was put together to suit that time of the year where we rush to a place where we might face the light again. Christmas more or less coincides with the winter solstice and then our hemisphere tilts once more towards the sun.

Again we have exploited the Advent Calendar theme. There is one story for each of the Advent days. Maybe you can enjoy them that way. Or maybe they are suitable for relaxing with after the festivities are over.

However you choose to read our collection, we hope you gain as much pleasure from the stories as we did working with the author who wrote them.

A Good Mechanic

Matthew Temple

Sam tossing a hot dog wrapper at Melissa's head, running up five steps to the pier, pastel blue railings dotted in rust, bumping into a woman in sweet floral dress crying – is that lady crying? – him sprinting too fast to be sure. Faster, run faster. *I win.*

Melissa muttering, "You ass, Samuel Johnson," but a big sea taking her words away, leaving thoughts. Those legs are too short for that body. His head's too big for his body. Samuel Johnson, you ass.

Melissa moving, her turn.

Patting her head until three fingertips find ketchup dabs on her fringe, cut geometric sharp last Monday, a lunchtime affair, less than one hour. Ketchup scabbing and Melissa hunting for a tissue in denim pockets so tight her fingers hurt going in and coming out even more but looking a million dollars. *Her opinion.* Are you pregnant or fat? Sam's opinion.

"I just washed it, you ass."

Back to her hair, big sea taking away her voice again. Melissa thinking – it's no good, shouting at high tide, he can't hear me. And there he is unchastened, still smiling, waving, goofy dancing on the pier. Okay you won. *You won, Sam.* Jesus, I'm twenty-four. I'm too old to race you, Samuel. You're too old to race, Samuel. My man Sam.

Come August, this Samuel Johnson is going to be her husband, Sam the goofy dancer, jubilant on a pastel pier. He's not inside her head so doesn't know she's too old to race, he's too old to race. Opening her mouth, cupping hands to echo, Melissa shouting, "I just fricking washed it, Sam," and this time, him reacting.

"Wash it again, you lazy doucher."

Up ahead, him laughing, pointing at fat waves humping the pier, he's been running past those pastel railings since his legs, way too short, began running, "I'll toss you in the sea if you keep moaning. Wash your wig, you lazy doucher."

Your laugh's too high for a man, her again. A little boy's voice with little boy's legs. Oh, Sam.

Two old ladies, carrying groceries between them, mundane pallbearers, Sam shouting "That girl wears a wig", running along his favourite pier to a small bar, run by Nathan, named after Nathan, to see Jack, his brother, two years younger, turning twenty this Fall. Jack, the Johnsons' baby. Jack, the army boy.

"Atten-shun!"

Six drinkers, looking to the door, seeing Sam. It's cold out there, a drinker is thinking, why the red face? Done wondering, going back to his beer, glass wet enough for a few gulps more, not knowing Sam was racing and winning all the way.

Jack pushing a seat from the table with his left foot, noticing a dust mark on his sneakers, nothing special, blue and white. Picking up a serviette, also not special, leaning to brush them clean, army habits in his young bones.

Then Jack remembering where he is, Nathan's on the pier, Sam looking at him with a silly grin, not brushing a sports shoe any more. Seconds later, pretending to tie an undone shoelace, fumbling in truth with a lace that's tight and neat. A precision shoelace. Army habit.

Crouching down at his lace, remembering Sam's dumb greeting. He does it every time. Why not say 'Hi' or 'Hello Jack'? Can't my brother act his age? He's twenty-two. I'm the baby, for crying out loud.

"Sit down, Sam."

9

The younger brother patting a free chair, creaky green and beaten, wanting to ask after Melissa. Thinking twice. Asking after Melissa, "No Mel?"

Sam rocking his seat, left right, table shaking "Easy, soldier. *Easy.* I ain't taking no orders from a ba-ba-baby."

Sam swigging Jack's drink, pushing out his tongue, mock horror, and belching, "Lemonade? Desert sun's made you soft. It'll be camel milk soon." Swigging again, swallowing, gasping, Jack tightening with impatience. Come on, come on. Where's Mel?

"Lazy Mel's still dragging her fat ass up here. Sorry, the *next Mrs Johnson's* still dragging her fat ass up here. Don't get her started on the wedding, Jackie Boy. What a con..."

Jack leaning over table, lowering voice, not smiling, never that, saying, "I told you, Sam. I'll chuck a few dollars in the hat."

Sam answering with a grunt.

"Cheers."

I'm the oldest, for Christ's sake. I don't want your dollars, ba-ba-baby. Sam thinking that on his creaking chair, left right. Nathan, fix your freaking creaking chair.

Sam rocking, looking at his fingernails, seeing grease a hundred bars of soap can't remove, feeling proud. I loves this grease, every speck. Telling himself dirty hands are a sign of a good mechanic. And so what if Steve let me go? Who needs Steve Malone? Lazy junkie. Plenty more garages need good mechanics. People drive in tough times and good times. People drive all the time. Only a matter of time. What's it been, a month?

Melissa walking over, passing the drinker back to wondering why the boy's face, Sam's that is, was red on a day like today.

"Why run off? Why dick about? And what was all that wig shit?"

Sam laughing again but nobody listening, Melissa smoothing her hair.

"Hello, Jack."

Melissa hugging Jack, kissing his cheek close to a small mole left of his lips, soft brown, thinking it's cute. Sam not thinking his brother's mole is cute. Skin cancer or black death or a bull's eye for a desert sniper that's what he calls it depending on his mood. His mood depends on many things, beer, sleep, work. When work comes, it comes by the hour, people always need a good mechanic, don't they? Will you look at my hands.

Jack moving to the bar trying not to move like an army man but his walk gives him away and after a few steps, he stops pretending he isn't an army man, a man who fires bullets at strangers in strange lands nobody cared about when he was a boy, two years younger than Samuel.

Walking straight, now, shoulders back, arms by sides, proud to be in his father's regiment. Peter Johnson, dying before his baby learned to march. Are you proud, Dad?

"Beer?"

"Yup."

"Not you. Mel. Beer, Mel?"

Melissa nodding, smiling and nodding, not caring about work, her new job, two months old, ten minutes from the army base. It began first week in April round the time Jack came home. First tour over and he came home.

Sorting paperwork, answering phones, in a long thin office smelling of burnt plastic, Melissa's new job. Boss is a realtor called Patricia with big spun hair, smoking and singing all day, sounding like bad jazz to Melissa. Shut up. Shut up. Get your terrible singing out of my ears. Can't you see I need to think?

11

Job boring but wedding looming. I'm going to be Mrs Melissa Johnson, playing it round her mouth at night, alone. I'm going to marry my man Sam.

"Why there?"

That's what Sam was asking when she took the job in a town with no pier. He had a point. Thirty minute bus ride there, thirty minute bus ride home. I like a change of scene, she kept saying, and the bus ride is okay. Listening to music, reading magazines, thinking about *our* wedding, yours and mine, Melissa and Sam. The Johnsons.

Sam beaming when he hears that, still beaming when his future wife goes to make fresh coffee, a treat for her man. But Melissa stopping at the kitchen door, motorcycle parts everywhere, forgetting fresh coffee, his treat, going to bed, reading alone.

Sam jumping on the bed. Stop ignoring me! God gave us tongues for a reason. Talk to me, Melissa. Grabbing her book, waggling his tongue in her face, she smelling his saliva. Same every time. Melissa enjoys reading on her bus ride to work.

Jack walking back from the bar. Everyone drinking, two people thinking what to say.

"How's the bike, Sam?"

"The *motorcycle*? She's beautiful. She's the best. She's my girl."

"She's all over my kitchen, that's how she is, Jack. All over my kitchen and my balcony. We eat on our knees. My kitchen table isn't a table. It's a pile of junk."

Sam leaping up, throttling Melissa, softly no harm done, playing a game.

"Junk! Hah! I know every one of those bolts by name. I'm their daddy."

Sam's motorcycle is a Triumph. Built in 1983 and bought ten years later, when Peter Johnson, fresh home

12

from another desert, needs to feel full of blood again. It's yours when I die, he's telling Sam over a Sunday beer, Sam's favourite kind, him and his father and beer. You're the family mechanic, Sam. Always tinkering even as a boy, you were, Sam. Nuts and bolts everywhere. You're the mechanic, Jack's the soldier.

Sam leaning back, creaking, telling his brother about his beloved machine. How he's stripping her engine, stripping her gas tank, removing her rear brake, rebuilding her wheels. Can you rebuild wheels? asks Jack. Sam shaking his head, going on with words so fast and familiar, sounding like a chant to his brother.

Sam stops talking, sudden as anything, looking under the table, turning to Jack.

"Easy tiger. None of your funny stuff today, thank you."

Jack blushing, Don't look at me, Mel. You'll guess. He'll guess. What have I done? Please don't look at me, Mel. Look away. Look away.

Melissa looking confused.

"My ba-ba-baby bro' was playing footsie with me. With his own brother. Join the Navy, soldier boy."

Sam drinking beer, spilling drops, going on with his tale of engines, gas tanks and wheels. Across the table Melissa sobbing, his future wife, head in hands, saying, "You and your stupid motorcycle," quiet as if the big sea's there in Nathan's bar, taking her voice away, "You and your stupid motorcycle."

About the author:
Matthew Temple was shortlisted in the Bridport Prize 2014. He lives in London.

A Reluctant Witness

Tracy Davidson

Dead men tell no tales. Well, the one lying on the floor by the counter certainly won't be telling any.

I hardly dare breathe for fear the perpetrator will hear me. Having killed the shopkeeper, now he's busy pistol-whipping the shopkeeper's wife, trying to make her tell him the combination to the safe.

There's absolutely nothing I can do to help her. Crouched down behind the fruit and veg, I'm too far away to tackle him. Anyway, he's twice my size. And armed.

There's no way I can get to the front door either without him noticing. He must have thought the shop was empty at this time of night, having locked the door when he came in.

This guy won't want to leave any witnesses alive. The wife is dead even if she does give up the combination. So will I be if he catches sight of me.

Of all the rotten times for my mobile phone to be out of juice. I was going to top it up when I paid for my shopping. All I can hope for is that one or other of the owners managed to hit an alarm button before the attack started. Or that a passer-by looks in and notices something wrong.

The wife finally stops her pitiful crying. I risk a quick peep over a box of oranges. It's all I can do not to scream out in horror at what is left of the poor woman. This guy definitely has anger issues. I blink tears away as I slowly slink back to the floor, trying to make myself as small and inconspicuous as possible.

The killer is breathing heavily now, and he's still angry. I hear him kicking things over and cursing. I pray he doesn't come back here for any reason. However much money he got out of the cash register, it's clearly not enough to satisfy him. It certainly can't be worth two lives.

I can hear sirens now, in the distance. The killer must hear them too, as he's stopped his rampage. I risk another peep. I shouldn't have done. He happens to be looking in my direction and senses my slight movement. His eyes glare straight into mine.

The sirens are louder now, getting ever closer. He takes a few steps forward, toward me, then stops. He raises his gun and points it right at me. I don't even bother trying to duck back down again. There's no point. For a moment we just stare at each other. Part of me wishes he would just hurry up and pull the trigger and be done with it.

But, to my surprise, he lowers the gun and grins. In a strange kind of way, the grin is even more menacing than anything else he's done this evening.

The sirens are deafening now. It breaks the hypnotic stare. He turns his back on me, vaults the counter and runs into the back room. I hear a door banging behind him. I stand up slowly, badly cramped muscles making me wince.

Police cars screech to a halt in front of the store. I raise my hands above my head and keep very still. I have somehow managed not to get shot by the bad guy. I don't want to get accidentally shot by the good guys now the immediate danger is over.

My eyes drift to the security camera above the shop counter. Even I can see it's not actually attached to anything. It's just there for show. My witness statement is going to be the only description of the killer. I'm the only one who can identify him. Which means the danger I'm in isn't over after all.

15

I can feel myself start to tremble, the delayed shock getting the better of me. I feel tears on my cheeks as police officers force their way in.

"He... he went out the back," I say, so softly they don't hear me the first time. I repeat the words and point the way.

One of the officers bends down to the dead woman to check for a pulse. A futile gesture.

His younger partner takes one look at the bloody pulp that was once a face, and heaves. That's enough to set me off, and before I know it I'm on my knees, heaving and sobbing, leaving a trail of snot and vomit on the already messed up floor.

Another officer is by my side in an instant, offering me comfort. He helps me to stand and I let him lead me out of the store, away from the carnage. Someone puts a blanket around my shoulders as a paramedic checks me over.

"Did you see him clearly, Ma'am?" the officer asks. "Can you give us a description?"

I hesitate before answering. Then I shake my head. "No," I say, "I only saw him briefly, from behind. Then I hid. I was too frightened to look. There's CCTV isn't there?"

The officer grimaces. "It wasn't hooked up," he said. "Did you notice if he was wearing gloves?"

I have to think about it. I nod. No fingerprints then. The killer may have been drugged up to his eyeballs, but he wasn't completely stupid. He came prepared.

The activity around me is a blur of noise and flashing lights, making my head ache. My statement, the truth rather heavily edited, is taken, and after being given a clean bill of health, I'm free to go. The nice officer who comforted me when I was sick arranges a ride home for me. They'll need to talk to me again, he says, but for now I should try and get a good night's sleep. Right. Like that's going to happen. After what I've seen tonight I wonder if I'll ever sleep well again.

The lights are all off when I get home. I see the tall frame of my brother briefly peeping out from behind the living room curtain. He must be worried about why I'm so late home. And why I've turned up in a police car.

I trudge up the path, my heart heavy. My brother doesn't come to the door until the police car has gone. He has an inherent distrust of the police. He has an inherent distrust of most people. Except for me. Even though I'm the younger sibling, by several years, I've spent most of my life watching out for him, rather than the other way around. And, it seems, going by tonight's events, I've not done a very good job of it.

He opens the door and retreats into the dark living room. I follow him slowly, wondering what kind of mood he's in. He has his back to me when I enter, so it's difficult to judge. I don't say anything, just put the lights on and wait for him to turn around.

When he finally does, I relax a little. The madness that was in them earlier has left his eyes. The drugs have worn off, thank goodness. I both love and hate my brother, in equal measure. I love him when he's clean, despite the trouble he seems to magnetically attract.

But I hate the monstrous thing he becomes when he goes on a bender. The thing that steals from me, menaces me, even beat me savagely once. He swore after that he would change. And he tried, I know he really tried. He was doing better. Until tonight anyway. I've no idea what, if anything, set him off this time.

Now, he's a double murderer. And I came close to

17

making it a hat-trick of victims. He rarely recognises me when he's that high. Which is why I thought he would kill me too.

At last, I break the awkward silence between us.

"Why?" is all I say. I have neither the energy nor the inclination to say anything else.

He shrugs. He looks confused. I wonder if he even remembers all the things he did. Does he remember the woman's cries as he beat the life out of her? Her pleas for mercy? When I see the tears on his face and the tremor in his hand as he reaches out to me, I know that he does.

Despite the abhorrence I feel at what he's done, despite how tired I am at having to clear up his messes, I go to him, take his hand and pull him into an embrace. He sobs on my shoulder, like the innocent little boy he once was, so long ago.

I don't know what the future holds for us. If the police ever track him down, the best he can hope for is life without parole. If I don't turn him in, I'll be an accessory to two murders, possibly get sent down for life too. I should do the right thing, for both our sakes. And for those poor people who lost their lives. But, as usual, I won't. He's the only family I have left. I can't betray him. And I won't.

About the author:
Tracy Davidson lives in Warwickshire, England, and enjoys writing poetry and flash fiction. Her work has appeared in various publications and anthologies, including: *Mslexia, Atlas Poetica, Writing Magazine, Modern Haiku, The Right-Eyed Deer, A Hundred Gourds* and *Roundyhouse*. Apart from writing, Tracy enjoys reading crime novels, photography, entering competitions, and travel.

A Sort of Artist

Don Nixon

The opening of the Early Renaissance exhibition was a success. Everyone who mattered was there – Wall Street movers and shakers, the fashionable Fifth Avenue crowd and the usual clutch of critics, poseurs, free loaders and self-arbiters of taste. Even *Vanity Fair* had sent a photographer – the ultimate seal of approval.

I stood sipping my glass of flat champagne in front of the little wooden panel of Sandro Del Campo's version of the Annunciation. Behind me two critics were in full voice. I winced as the pitch went higher. It reminded me of the old days when Joan Sutherland and Marilyn Horne were at the Met, trading high notes in some showy Rossini cabaletta.

I caught Carlo's eye and he winked at me. He is far too handsome to be a capo di capo in Palermo. Most of the Mafiosi of his rank have pasta heavy bellies and jowls like Mussolini but Carlo is as slim as the angel announcing the good news to the Virgin in the Del Campo picture. Michelangelo would have drooled over him as a model and I was hoping to persuade him to pose for me when the exhibition was over, he had half promised. I could see him as a Fallen Angel. It was the darkness at the back of his eyes that I wanted to try and capture.

"It is so typical of Del Campo. See the twist of curl at the angel's neck," trilled one of the critics. "Could almost be a Durer."

"Or even Titian," said his companion, not to be outdone as a small group gathered, eager to be told what to admire. "He must have been an influence on Titian. It's clearly one of Del Campo's later more mature works.

19

Look at the halo. He's using that Venetian trick of adding Murano powdered glass to the paint. You can see the light coming through. It is quite seminal."

I could only agree. Each feature they had mentioned was typical of Del Campo's late style. And I should know. I had spent nearly a year studying Del Campo's work. I glanced at the little crowd around the picture. Already they had picked up the right phrases and I heard murmurings of 'curl', 'angel', 'Durer', 'Titian'.

"Who is Murano?" I heard a visitor from Wisconsin whisper.

I smiled and looked across again at the capo. He was pleased. His investment was paying off. This was the icing on the cake. Would they be gaping so reverentially, I wondered, if they knew that this 'Annunciation' was not the work Sandro Del Campo, born Mantua, Italy 1399, profession painter and friar, but by me Alastair Fraser, born Leith, Scotland 1975, profession painter and forger.

Even as a small child I could draw. I loved copying the pictures in the books at school and I made pocket money painting pictures from old photographs in family albums. Inevitably I ended up in an Art Department which was the poor relation in a Polytechnic with aspirations to becoming a university. We were the ones who were stuck in the demountables while the engineers had the run of the new buildings. But I have come a long way since leaving Art School. I had soon realised that my skill in precise representational painting was not going to make much money. At that time, abstract expressionism was the vogue and pulling in the big bucks and crowding all the gallery space. I did not want to teach but I had to eat and so I found myself making a modest living doing quick charcoal portraits for tourists outside the National Gallery and selling meticulously crafted copies of Old Masters which were very popular with American visitors.

I had just sold a good copy of a Raphael Madonna to a matron from Illinois when I became aware of a man watching me. This was the man who was to change my life. Count Emilio Barrata.

Barrata is a leading international expert on Italian Renaissance Art. He is a highly respected dealer with galleries in Rome, Florence, London and New York and as I was to discover a member of the top family in the Palermo Mafia with a links to the Neapolitan Camorra. One of the true aristocrats of international crime his lineage is ancient and impeccable.

"You have talent young man," he said in his heavily accented English. "Almost genius as a copyist but no originality or creativity I think. You are what I would rate a sort of artist. Like a superior draughtsman."

I flushed. It was not the first time I had heard this judgement on my work. At Art School it had been the constant refrain of my tutors. 'A glorified draughtsman' one of them had sneered. I had come to accept it but it had rankled.

"You must be happy with it," said Count." This is a rare talent. Let me help you use it."

He waved his hand dismissively at my departing American customer.

"Not from the pittance you get from the likes of her. Young man, I can make you very rich."

I listened and that was how I came to join the upper echelon of the criminal classes.

Of course it took time. I had a lot to learn about mixing period paint and working over daubs on ancient canvases. The Count had access to discarded old canvases and centuries old wood panels and a vast knowledge of the pigments used by Renaissance artists. The main problem was not the technicalities but getting into the mind-set of the painter I was copying. I had to learn to think like him.

As the Count often says, "Empathy is the hallmark of the great forger."

And I have it.

For over a year, I studied the fifteenth Century painters in the galleries and private collections that the Count and the capo arranged for me to visit. Finally I was ready for my first job. Carlo, the capo, sent me his good wishes and the present of a Ferrari. It made me smile as I wondered what my uncle Hamish would have said if he had lived to see his despised 'poncy arty farty nephew' working for the Mafia. Uncle Hamish was a self-proclaimed hard man who was an enforcer for one of the Glasgow drug gangs in the 1980s. Fond of using his fists and the word 'respect', he had made my young life a misery when he was out of jail. It was a pity he had died of overindulgence in the goods he peddled. It would have been a pleasure to demand 'respect' now from that drunken sot though I suppose I get my criminal genes from him.

The working of the scam was simple but it depended on two things. The copy had to be exact and that was my province. Secondly, and this was the key to the whole operation, the forgery had to be authenticated by an international art expert and this was where the Count came in. Such was his standing in the Art World no one was likely to question his judgment. It was an ideal combination.

For my first outing, the capo arranged for an original painting to be stolen. It was a charming little Nativity canvas by Firanesi owned by an oil man in Houston. A ransom was demanded. The owner was warned that if he went to the police then the painting would be destroyed. As the ransom was moderate, the owner chose to pay. It was cheaper than the hike in insurance would be on his other paintings if he went to the police. I then made a copy which was returned to the owner. The Count certified it was the original and it was returned to its pride of place in the oil man's collection.

The real money was made from the sale of the stolen original. The Count has a list of wealthy collectors who are willing to spend millions buying stolen masterpieces. They have what the Count dismisses as 'art addiction'. It is a disease. In mansions all over the world there are secret rooms containing stolen paintings. Only the new owners will ever see them and that seems to be the buzz they get from them. The capo has quite a collection in his villa in Palermo. One of them is a Raphael. It was stolen from the Vatican in the nineteenth Century. The forgery was done by the legendary Van Helm who worked for the capo of the time. It was the beginning of the deceptions and I am the latest in the long line of Mafioso forgers. It is the Raphael forgery which is now in the Vatican. Van Helm was never caught and no one outside the business has ever heard of him but his forgeries are all over the world in galleries and collections. My ambition was to be the new Van Helm.

I was a little disappointed when I saw the real Raphael in the capo's villa. It is an early work by Raphael and I think I prefer the Van Helm forgery which in subtle ways seems to have concentrated in it all the later elements of the mature Raphael's genius. Was Van Helm then a greater artist than Raphael?

It is an interesting question. There is so much bullshit in the Art world. Who decides what counts as great Art? In my opinion Van Helm was as good as and at times greater than the artists whose work he forged. To my mind, the Vatican got the better of the transaction. The forgery is the better picture. Over the years, like Van

Helm, I have sometimes 'improved' some of the drearier religious paintings the Count has brought to me. From an aesthetic point of view I am doing the owners and the world of art a service. The owner gets back a better picture than the one stolen even if he does not realise it. What is great art then? Is it just what the experts tell us?

And so our business prospered and as the Count had promised, I became a very rich man.

The system was not totally fool-proof but the capo was always there to iron out any little difficulties. There was one occasion when the owner who, had once quarrelled with the Count for political reasons, wanted another expert to authenticate my forgery. I had been too clever. The original was a domestic subject of a woman with a cat. It was by a second rate artist, good of its kind, but derivative. I had made a slight improvement to the fur at the cat's neck which another expert might have noticed. I told the capo who was amused that Barrata hadn't spotted it before it was returned and he arranged a convenient road accident for the owner. The forgery perished in the flames with the owner so all was well. There were no loose ends left and we retained the original.

But last year I was getting restless. I was becoming bored with just copying. The Count's remark at our first meeting about my lack of creativity and the attitude of my tutors at Art School all those years ago still rankled. I decided that I would try to create my own painting in the style of an old master and see if it could be passed off as a new discovery. This time it would not only be the Count as judge but authentication would be thrown open to all the experts. I was determined to show the Count that I could do more than just copy. I suppose also that I wanted to prove to myself that I could go one better than Van Helm.

So I took a year off and studied everything I could find about a little Mantuan friar called Sandro Del Campo. In his *Lives of the Artists*, the sixteenth century art historian Vasari had written about Del Campo's painting of the Annunciation but it had disappeared during the French invasions of Italy. Vasari had spoken of the technique as foreshadowing that of Leonardo so it could have been an important picture in the History of Art. I would recreate it.

Its discovery had to be plausible. The capo arranged for it to be 'found' during alterations being made to his cousin's villa in Mantua near where it was known that Del Campo had spent most of his life in the local friary. The scene of the discovery was beautifully staged – a work of performance art in itself. The Count was in his element in the international TV coverage that followed. It was the biggest event in the Art World for years.

So that is how I came to be standing in front of my Annunciation in that New York Gallery. The capo was thrilled. As it was found on his cousin's property, the Family would make millions out of it on the legitimate market and the Count had found a new career as a TV celebrity that fuelled his enormous ego. However, I felt curiously flat. I had an overwhelming urge to shout the truth.

"Listen you idiots," I wanted to yell. "I painted this masterpiece. I did it. Alastair Fraser. I'm not just as good as old Sandro. I'm better."

But I didn't. I remembered my mansion in Tuscany, my latest Porsche, my yacht and all the beautiful women I could buy and I stayed silent. I had made my Mephistophelian compact with the Count too well and there was no going back. Still I knew the truth and I had proved to myself that I was a real artist. That would have to be enough. At any rate Fedora, my current mistress, thinks so.

25

I glanced along the wall at other genuine paintings. My eye was taken by a study by Mantegna of *Joseph in the Carpenter's Shop*. The perspective was stunning. It took my breath away. What could have just been a geometrical study in lesser hands was alive. Yet my perspective is just as good. As I gazed at the picture, I felt a strange affinity with Mantegna. It was the technical virtuosity. Van Helm must have felt the same about Raphael I thought.

I had found a new challenge. It all seemed to suddenly come together. I was on the threshold of a new career. I would no longer copy. I would create. In future I would choose my own subject material. I had been half way there with the Del Campo but I still had to use the subject matter of the vanished original painting. Now I would choose my own subject material. This was further than Van Helm had gone. Great as he was, he still was basically a copyist.

I was excited. I need no longer be confined to the Renaissance period. During World War Two, many paintings had disappeared, looted by the Nazis, and no records survived. It would be easy. With the capo's resources, arranging discoveries would be feasible and there would not be the problem of ancient canvases and authentic paint materials as with the Renaissance painters. I smiled. It would even be a way of getting my own back on those Art School fools who had sneered at my efforts at expressionism when I was a student. What would be their reaction if they ever were to find out that the abstract they or others had authenticated as a lost Klee or Modigliani was a Fraser? The painting part of it would be easy. Reproducing the cubism of a Braque would be child's play compared to coping with the intricacies and sophistication of a Del Campo. At a late stage in my career when I was rich enough to be untouchable, I might even own up to the forgeries. It would blow the pretensions of the Art World apart.

That was for the future. For the time being I needed to focus on Mantegna. Below the gallery the Count was finishing yet another TV interview. This time it was a Chinese media company. Now there was a potential market to be sure and trust the Count to smell it out. China was opening up to the West and this might be the way in for the Cosa Nostra. I rang the Count on my cell phone.

"Emilio I want you to dig up all you can about Mantegna. Find out if he ever did a Flight into Egypt? If he didn't, then I have a great idea for the donkey and using the pyramids for perspective. Fedora will be perfect as the model for Mary. The capo can arrange for a cousin to do some excavations at another villa for the discovery."

I walked over to the capo. He'd make a marvellous model for Pharaoh. There is an incipient cruelty in the curve of the lip.

"You are going to like this," I began.

About the author:
Don Nixon has been writing for about twelve years. He has had had a number of short stories and poems published in anthologies and magazines in the UK, North America and Italy His first short story was published by Tindal Street Press – *Birmingham Noir* in 2002. More recently he had two short stories published in the Bridge House crime anthology *Crime After Crime,* and a short story on a Shakespearean theme will be published later this year in an anthology arising from the Canterbury Festival. This year two poems have been published by Offa's Press in the anthology *Poetry of Shropshire.* His novel *Ransom* was published last year.

After the Commodores

Jesse Falzoi

Angie was the only one in San Jose who had neither car nor licence. She used to page me in the evening, and half an hour later I rang the doorbell at Black Rose's house on South Side. She was still wearing her night gown. I had my breathing on hold to get used to the smell of perfume, wonder trees and her body, and said, "What's up?"

She grinned. Hardly reaching my shoulders she weighed at least a hundred and sixty. She had a double chin and the small eyes of a pig. Her hair, damaged from uncountable perms and colouring, needed half a bottle of spray to stay in shape. All men were crazy about Angie, but she went for blacks only.

"I've got a new job," she said. "Let's celebrate."

"Cool," I said. "Can I work there, too?" My car was a gas-guzzler. I was slowly running out of money and I still had five weeks to cover before flying home. There was always my credit card, and there was always Steve, but he had his plans about the both of us, and I had mine.

We drove to Cougars. A tall guy with a base cap asked me if I wanted to dance. I said that I never danced with strangers, but he knew that I talked to strangers if they paid for my beer. "I know you." He smiled and said, "You're the European."

I told him that I felt like driving to the beach. His eyes were fixed on the dance floor where a couple was dancing to the Chi-Lites. They hardly moved at all as if they were about to sleep.

"I love that song," the guy said.

"So?" I said.

He put his half-full bottle onto the table. "Let's get out of here."

I steered my car though the deserted town, heading west. There were high concrete walls on both sides of the winding road, marked with traces of car paint in all colours. Every now and then we passed a dried-up wreath that was hanging beneath a photo of a smiling man or woman. I pushed the start button of my tape player.

"Fuck Burdon," the guy said.

I turned up the volume and slammed on the gas. "It's your people he's playing with now," I said.

"Easy, woman," the guy said, putting his hand on my thigh.

"What's your name?"

Grinning, he said, "Eric."

I parked next to the beach and asked him if he felt like taking a walk. He climbed onto the backseat. "All Germans want to come here and drive around in an old American car."

I looked at him through the rear view mirror. I looked at his black skin on my ruby leather. "It's a pimp's car," Angie had said, when I'd picked her up the first time. "In the seventies, pimps drove such cars," she'd said. "Nobody would drive such a car today."

Eric said, "It's their once-in-a-lifetime thing."

I changed the tape and started to roll a reefer. Before I had left home, I had spent weeks mixing tapes. I didn't have a plan what to do, but I knew that I would buy a car, and that I would drive on highways, and that I would listen to these tapes.

Eric gently took the reefer out of my hand. "Having the moments of their lives in the big fucking States of America." He inhaled deeply and leaned back. "Fucking big black guys at the beach," he said, passing the reefer back to me.

"The grass here is a thrill," I said.

He stroked my neck, and then rested his chin on my shoulder. "What are you waiting for?"

Eric lit one of my cigarettes, rolled down the window and checked on his face in the side mirror. He scratched his head and yawned.

"Where do you live?" I asked.

"Just drive," he said and turned on the radio to some R'n'B station.

We shared my last chewing gum and headed back. He said "turn right" and "turn left after the next intersection", and then, on King Road, in front of a prefab home, put his hand on my thigh again. "See ya."

I felt them there, sleeping in their beds. His big family who would have breakfast in a few hours. Cereals, fluffy white peanut butter sandwiches, half a gallon of low fat milk on the big table. And him sitting on a chair in the corner, drinking coffee, yawning.

"See ya," I said.

Steve was washing down his vitamins with orange juice when I got back. I quickly walked by and locked myself in the bathroom.

He knocked at the door.

I looked into the mirror thinking that I was looking at a woman who had just fucked a big black American.

"Talk to me, please," Steve said.

I went under the shower. When I came out of the bathroom he had left.

Later, at one of the happy hour places on Market Street I went to the bar to get two beers while Angie filled our plates at the buffet.

"You gotta get out of that place," she said and put a huge bowl of Cesar salad onto the table.

I shrugged. "I don't have the money."

She was nibbling at a chicken wing. The juice was running down her fingers. "We'll find you a job," she said.

The men at the next table had been watching us. They had paid for our second beer. Smiling, we raised the cold bottles. They joined us after a while, but since they were white Angie was in a hurry to leave.

In her room, there was a bed, a closet and a sideboard full of cosmetics, hair products, and cheap perfumes. She threw a bunch of dresses and skirts onto her unmade bed. "You're cute, you know," she said, "but you gotta show it, too."

I reached for a black dress. "How about that?"

"Too sophisticated," she said.

Her head slightly bent, she was watching me slipping in and out of her clothes. Sometimes she made a knot here or pulled the fabric there but let go in the end. "Let's do some shopping," she said.

I watched her putting on fake nails. "I'm going back next month," I said. "It doesn't make sense."

She held her hands up, waiting for the cherry polish to dry. "Back where?"

We were getting ready, when Black Rose knocked on the door. "Ladies," he said, lying down on Angie's bed.

"What's up?

She crawled next to him. "Rita's looking for a place to stay."

He let her take a drag from his reefer. Her skin was even lighter than mine. Their legs next to each other looked like giant piano keys.

"The guy she's living with is a jerk," Angie said.

I sat down on the floor and leaned back against the wall.

Black Rose bent over, passing me the reefer. "What's it like in good ole Germany?"

I was getting high. "Germany?" I said. "Where the fuck is Germany?"

"We gotta find someone to marry you," Angie said. "You suck dick a couple of times, and then you'll get a divorce."

"All right," I said.

She reached for her cigarettes. "We won't let you go, honey."

Black Rose looked at my legs. "You can have the room across the hall," he said. "We'll put some paint on and maybe get a new carpet. How's that?"

I knew that Angie didn't lock her door when she couldn't pay the rent. I returned the reefer, smiling. "When can I move in?"

We were sitting in the backyard next to the pool that hadn't been filled with water for a decade. Instead it housed broken fridges, washing machines, and heaps of garbage bags. It was eight o'clock in the morning, so the sun was still having mercy on us. We'd just come home.

Angie had swiped two Coronas from Black Rose's fridge. "He's mad at me anyway," she said, glancing at the windows behind which everybody was still sleeping. "He blames me for the last phone bill."

Two days ago I had called my parents in Germany. They had told me that my boyfriend was planning to pick me up at the airport. I had told them a lot of things, but I hadn't told them that I was planning to stay. "What if he kicks you out?" I said.

She stretched her legs and said, "There are rooms all over town."

I held the cold bottle against my thigh. "You're sure?"

She got rid of her tight dress. I'd often felt too fat at the beach and had sat there without taking my clothes off. Angie seemed comfortable everywhere, naked or not. "You're too serious," she said and lit one of her menthols.

"Am I?"

She blew rings into the air that was getting warmer every minute. "Like all Germans."

A friend of Angie's knew a guy selling green cards. We picked him up in front of a KFC. In front of a villa that looked as if it had been flown over from the Mediterranean, he told me to park the car. "Wait here," he said.

I watched him crossing the street. He looked like a college guy who wanted to get the assign papers of a friend because he had missed a class. "The airplane is leaving in ten minutes," I said.

"What airplane?"

"The one supposed to bring me home."

Angie turned on the radio and searched for a station until the Commodores filled the car. "You are home," she said.

"And if he just told shit?"

She sang, "*That's why I'm easy.*"

I turned down the volume. "I will be illegal. Actually,

I'm illegal now."

"*Easy like Sunday morning,*" Angie sang, turning up the volume again.

The guy stepped out of the villa and gave us a sign to come in. Entering the hall, I felt like in a movie. The cleaning lady must have left only minutes ago. We went to the second floor where a young kid with a military cap was waiting for us. He was wearing shoddy sweatpants and a shirt he probably hadn't changed in a week. "How's it going?" he said, extending his tiny hand.

I was taken aback by its cold. I wasn't used to something being cold anymore, except for beer bottles. "All right," I said.

"You can call me Mahler," he said.

We followed him into his room. The curtains were drawn and the only light came from a floor lamp. "Like the composer?" I said.

"No," he said, "Like the *Horst* Mahler." He looked at me and said, "So you want to be American?"

I cleared my throat. "Well."

Angie said, "You're right, kiddo." She let herself fall back onto the mattress that was lying on the floor. Apart from a desk there was no other furniture. The kid and Angie's friend sat down on cardboard boxes. We weren't allowed to smoke inside, but we were forced to gulp half a dozen Tequila shots. I was drunk pretty soon and sank down next to Angie who was holding a cigarette without lighting it.

Mahler was fumbling with his cap. He was talking about Che Guevara and communism, and how he had believed in the GDR where he once had a penfriend, and how disappointed he had been when this penfriend had moved to Munich for a better job after the revolution. He liked to say the word revolution. He said *ree-volution* with a pause after the first syllable. Then he jumped up and said, "Got the picture?"

Angie searched my bag and took out the envelope that the man at Foto Express had given me this morning. The picture was wrapped in my last savings. Black Rose wouldn't expect the rent before Friday next week, but I was getting ready to leave my door open for him.

Mahler stuffed the envelope into his cap and put it back on. "I'd do it for free, but you got to have principles."

As we were heading downtown again Angie's friend told us that Mahler's father was a fundamentalist republican, who saw himself as a crusader against illegal immigration. Angie's friend had told Mahler that my father had been a famous member of the SED. He'd also told him that my father was one of the few who were against the reunification.

"I grew up on the other side of the wall," I said.

The guy grinned. "Commies get it for half price."

Three days later I had my green card. Angie and I went to Cougars to celebrate. "Miss America," Angie said, "Got any plans?"

I ordered two beers. "The sky is the limit," I said.

I stayed at the bar to keep an eye on the entrance. Angie was asked to dance. A couple of songs later she wanted to go to a party, but I said no.

She hugged me, saying, "You're not mad at me if I go?"

"I'm not," I said.

"His friend is cute, though," she said. "You should come along." She stepped back to wave at somebody. The guys around us were staring at her tight velvet dress that would soon land on the floor of somebody's bedroom.

I kissed her on the mouth. "You have fun, honey."

My beer was nearly empty. I thought about ordering another one, when a man said, "I dig your style."

I liked it, too. I had skipped the fashion show today and put on my Levi's and an old, loose T-shirt.

"Can I get you something?" the man said.

I grinned. "If I don't have to listen to your stories."

He took my empty bottle and showed it to the girl behind the bar. "I don't have any," he said.

"Everybody does," I said.

"I like your Cadillac," the man said after a while.

I put my hand around the cold bottle. It was a Beck's.

The man held up his bottle and said, "It's German, isn't it?"

"Yeah," I said.

"I'd like to go there," he said.

I smiled. The bottle in my hand got warmer. I thought of the airport in Hamburg and the snow. I looked at the guy in his tank top. Perhaps he'd never seen snow before. Never picked it up to form a ball and then threw it. Never tasted it. Never felt it melting on the skin.

About the author:
Jesse Falzoi was born in 1969 in Hamburg and raised in Lübeck, Germany. After stays in the US and France, she moved to Berlin in the beginning of the nineties, where she still lives with her three children.

Her stories, as well as her translation of Donald Barthelme's *Sentence*, have appeared in American, Russian, German, Swiss, Irish and Canadian magazines and anthologies. Meet her at www.jessefalzoi.de

Air

Catrin Kean

I woke choking, like someone was pushing down on my chest. It was her thin arm, weighted with dreams. There wasn't enough air for the both of us and I had to get out. She smelled sour and sweet and she didn't wake when I pushed her away. Her moist hair tangled on the pillow. I gathered up my clothes and escaped to the kitchen.

Beer cans, an empty vodka bottle, takeaway food cartons overflowing with butt ends. It was like an oven in there with the sun poking spiteful fingers through the frayed curtains. I ran the tap and gulped down coffee-tasting water from a dirty mug. I was so dry I felt like I might crackle and burn, and I smelled rank. I couldn't remember whether we'd shagged. We had probably tried, or pretended, because we were both lost, two lone flies banging up against a window. I had to get out. I thought about leaving her a text but there was nothing to say. I deleted her number instead.

Outside, I swayed in the brightness of an ordinary day. There was a kite flying and a dog yapping and some kids running. Two women from the next door caravan were sitting on deck chairs talking. I sat on the steps and pulled my boots on. One of the women was crying and the other one said, "Look Sue, honest to god you're the strongest woman I've ever known and you're going to get through this." I walked through the caravan site past men reading newspapers and women stretched out on sunbeds and some kids taking turns on a skateboard. The sun was low and fierce. I felt enormous, like a giant striding through a toy town. I wished I hadn't smoked so much. I wish I'd drunk coffee before I'd left. I got into my car which was airless as a coffin, and sat there. "What now?" I asked Cal.

"Let's break the sound barrier," said Cal, from somewhere in my head.

I started the car up, wound down the windows and skidded down the narrow lane. Birds leapt from the hedges and branches bent and snapped and the car filled with leaves and clouds of little seeds and broken petals.

I met Cal when we were both working the night-shift shelf-stacking. The other kids were either a few vodkas short of a piss-up or students with put-on accents who kept reminding you they were geniuses really and only doing this job to pay for uni-varsity. But then there was this long-limbed kid with narrow dark eyes and a sarky sideways smile. Some of the student girls fancied him – girls always fall for that skinny floppy-haired look – but he wasn't having any of it. I liked him straight away. We took fag breaks together and listened to the same music and when he got sacked for pinching a packet of broken biscuits that they would have just chucked out anyway, I walked out with him. "Fuck you," we said in unison as we left. And that was that. Friends. Someone to go to gigs and get stoned with, or have a few pints with down the snooker club. Nothing complicated. And thinking back, I didn't really know much about him. Not the realness of him. I just knew what his favourite band was.

I drove Cal to his mother's funeral in Bristol. She'd lived there ever since leaving Cal and his dad when Cal was about ten. She ran off with some arty theatre guy and they did these fringe performances where they shouted at the audience and made them feel like shit, which you deserve if you've paid to see that kind of bollocks. Cal's mother was cool though, young-looking, and she always looked at you like she was about to tell you a secret which was kind of sexy though I never told Cal that. His dad was a twat or at least that's what Cal said.

Cal's mother dying was one of those shocking things that twists and turns in your head and that you can never untangle. It wasn't like cancer which you've got time to think about. It was one second to the next. She was on the motorway and her car – which it turned out the theatre guy had fixed himself – started smoking from under the bonnet, so she pulled over onto the hard shoulder and got out. And probably before she'd even had time to see it a lorry driver blasted her to bits. Just like that. She went from scrolling for the number of the RAC on her phone, to being not there.

I couldn't stop thinking about it but I didn't know how Cal felt because he never said. Sometimes I thought it might not be so bad. Your parents are supposed to die before you. I tried to imagine my mother dying and I thought I'd probably be a bit upset but to be honest she was a bit of an embarrassment with her pink wine and her shrieking and showing her friends baby photos of me in the bath when she was drunk. My life would definitely be quieter if she wasn't there. But Cal's mother already wasn't there: it wasn't like he'd physically miss her. Maybe he'd got over losing her years ago. Maybe he was fine.

We got stoned in the car driving to the funeral and Cal said it didn't matter because he'd already told them he wasn't carrying the coffin because he'd done his back in kick-boxing. Cal didn't do kick-boxing. We couldn't stop laughing about this as we sped down the motorway and Cal doing kick-boxing moves at the other cars and then we laughed more at people's blank faces as they looked back at him. I was scared I was going to laugh in the funeral too but then I saw the coffin all covered in flowers and I thought, she's inside there, and I didn't laugh any more and neither did Cal. Some guys in suits carried it into the church and the day became strange, all the colours hard and cold, like when there was an eclipse of the sun and the world looked like a photograph. Cal kept breathing in, short shallow breaths.

Cal's mother's friends irritated the shit out of me. They were the kind of people who smile when there's no-one to smile at, and they stood up and said things that meant nothing, like about what she'd contributed to fringe theatre and shit like that, and if I'd stood up and said she made you tingly when she looked at you it would have described her better but of course I couldn't. I kept looking at the coffin. It didn't make sense that Cal's mother with her faraway eyes was in there. Maybe she wasn't.

Some people cried. I was hoping we didn't have to sing that 'Abide With Me' song because it always gets me, even at my bastard uncle Ray's funeral. I pretended my nose was running to get rid of the evidence and I glanced at Cal to see if he'd noticed but he hadn't. He looked like he was a church statue made of plaster, and his mouth was a gash in his face and his eyes were blind as stones.

We went back to their house which smelled of cats and vegetables and if my mother'd been there she would have got the hoover out. There was some nasty-looking brown food which we didn't touch and loads of wine because these arty types drink like fish. The theatre guy drifted round the room with a dreamy smile thanking people and some of the women were showing what I thought was an unhealthy interest in Cal and disguising it as sympathy. Cal came to find me in the kitchen and said he couldn't fucking stand it so we pocketed some bottles of fair-trade wine and left. The theatre guy came to hug Cal. He had scrappy grey hair and he smelled of dust. He hugged Cal and got tears on his jacket. He said, "I'm so sorry Callum, you were her world," and Cal said, "Yeah yeah," and then when we got outside he said, "that guy's dim as fuck."

"Literally," I said.

And we cracked up.

We drove back to Wales wine-swigging spliff-smoking. There was a gash in the black clouds with the sky shining through and the evening was sparkling with car lights. "This is good stuff," said Cal, and he passed the spliff to me, and it was good stuff and I forgot his mother had died. But then we passed a woman broken down on the hard shoulder, standing beside her car looking back down the motorway. We both looked at her and time froze for a second, became a snapshot, just like the snapshot of the second before Cal's mother died. The image flared in my head and then burned out again and I knew that had happened to Cal as well and I thought he would say something and he did. He said, "All these fuckers paying six quid to get into Wales. We should come here at three in the morning with a fucking shotgun and empty the tills."

"Let's do it," I said. Cal rolled another spliff. We were approaching the bridge and the clouds had cleared and the air and the water were blue and gold and the sky looked like it went on forever. The bridge was silhouetted, solid, against it. Cal said, "It looks like a fucking harp or something." And it did, with the turquoise suspension cables as fine as strings. "Imagine the fuck-off music that thing would play," he said, and he air-guitared and more blank faces stared. I opened the window and put my foot down and when we went over the bridge it was like we

41

were flying and the car filled with blue and gold air and the sky burned and the two of us shouting at the sky.

I dropped him off at his dad's house and only then said, "Sorry about your mother." He hesitated. Then he said, "Yeah. It's mental as fuck."

"Literally," I said. I don't remember where this came from but we always said it and it always cracked us up but not this time.

My phone rang. It was a number I didn't recognise so it must have been her. I didn't answer it but immediately it rang again so I picked it up. I didn't speak.

"Hello?" she asked, in a small voice.

"Alright." I wished I hadn't answered. She was going to turn reproachful.

"I woke up and you'd gone." There was no answer to that and I wondered whether just to switch the phone off but she hadn't done anything to deserve that.

"I needed to get back."

"To see Callum?"

I was driving past the estuary, herds of ponies grazing on the salty grass. A broken boat caught in sludge.

"What?"

"It's just that you kept talking about him last night so I thought…"

I didn't remember talking about him. A car horn blasted. I'd driven across a roundabout and cut someone off. Fuck off, I mouthed at the woman's stupid outraged face.

"Hello?"

Something was moving inside me, heavy and shifting like floodwater. For some reason I thought of my mother, drinking with her friends. Her creased cleavage, bright lipstick, head thrown back laughing.

When something shit happens it doesn't feel shit all the time. Like when Cal's mother died, sometimes it felt like the most logical thing in the world. Of course she would break down on that day in that place and the lorry driver would be there waiting to smash into her. It was always going to happen and she must have known it and we should have known it too but we missed the signs.

But then this horror builds up inside you and it's so much that you panic, like choking, like being in a room with no air. Like nightmares.

I chucked the phone down and drove towards the motorway. The sky was golden. "Hello?" she said, "Hello?" Her voice tiny, faraway, lost in another place and time.

I didn't see so much of Cal after the funeral. I got a night shift job with an events catering company, serving crap food to pissed-up wankers who never said thank you. Cal started seeing some girl with a black fringe over her eyes who never spoke. She wasn't my type but he seemed happy enough. Then one night, just after I got home, stones at my window. I looked out; it was Cal, grinning in the darkness. "Oy bastard," he said, "come out and play."

We went and sat down on the dirty little beach. The sea was shifting and sucking on the shale and behind us the city sparkled like stars and the Saturday night rhythm riding on the wind. Stones trickled from the cliffs. Cal rolled a spliff and we sat shivering, smoking. He asked about the job. I said the boss was a twat but the other guys were cool, mainly Polish and African. I told him about one African guy who talked with a click click. "That's the language," I said. "It's called Xhosa. It's cool. Crazy as fuck."

"Literally," he said, but he didn't laugh and he seemed to have something on his mind but I never asked what it

43

was. We smoked till we got cold and then we went home and I was pretty stoned but as far as I can remember he was fine. But a few days later I was woken by my mother shouting at me to come down and I went and my mother was standing by the front door with her hand over her mouth and Cal's dad was standing there too and in his face I could see he had broken like a doll and could not be put back together, and I immediately understood. I knew everything and it was like all my life had been leading up to this day.

In the blue early morning Cal hitched a lift down the M4 to the place where it's just sky, to the bridge which plays fuck-off music as it flies over the vast expanse of slow-motion water. He climbed onto the barrier and stretched his arms out and allowed the wind to take him. He twisted through the air graceful as a diver and breathed it in, deep into his lungs, deep into his body, until air was all there was left of him, until the monstrous river closed his lungs forever.

"He wouldn't have suffered," said Cal's dad, who didn't seem to be such a twat after all. "He would have been unconscious before he hit the water."

Unconscious. Wiped clean.

It must have felt like flying.

I stayed in bed on the day of the funeral. My mother went. I heard her footsteps on the stairs when she came back and I was thinking of all the things I didn't want her to say. "He had a lovely send off." "The hymns were beautiful." "People wondered where you were." She came in and hesitated in the doorway. Then she walked to the window and opened it.

"D'you want a cup of tea?"

"Alright."

She walked out again but paused in the doorway.

"If you had something on your mind," she said, "you'd talk to me about it, wouldn't you?"

"Yeah," I said.

Like fuck I would.

And then she was gone and I heard her boiling water in the kitchen and I wished she'd told me what it was like and what hymns they'd sung and who'd asked after me.

I never knew what grief was like because Cal never said, but I thought I should probably get up and go to the pub and sit in the corner with a pint. So I did, nodding at the guys who hovered awkwardly, mumbling "sorry mate." I also realised – a definite bonus – that a man in mourning is very attractive to women. I planned to miss Cal in this way for a good few months.

But then it hit me, a ferocious choking thing, physical, nearer to fury and jealousy and hate than to love. And I didn't miss him because he wasn't gone. He was behind me in the shadows. He was a step in front of me on the street, his face turned away. He was in my dreams, playing the blue strings of the bridge, up in the sky with the demons. He taunted me; he had stepped off the bridge into eternity, knew everything there was to know, and I knew nothing. I was just a man lying face down on the pavement, tasting dust.

I drove past the burning city of Port Talbot. A speed camera flashed somewhere behind me but I didn't slow down. Down past Cardiff, spires in the sky. A jam ahead, roadworks or something. I speeded up a slip-road to avoid it. The city skidded past. A cat streaked across the road in front of me. Bright shops, blurred, and some bare-legged giggling girls with heels like snooker cues. I'd taken a wrong turning, didn't know the way back to the motorway. Shit. Fucking shit.

There was a hot night wind blowing in from the sea. There were old men gossiping on benches and gleaming girls leaning into gleaming cars. There was reggae on the wind and a smell of spice. There were betting shops and takeaways and barbers and pawn shops and late night mini markets and halal butchers and there was Cal's mother walking.

Cal's mother walking. She looked like she was dressed up for some performance, tall in a long lacy dress and a fur coat and jewellery, unearthly, a goddess walking through the feverish city, discarded takeaway cartons at her feet. I slammed on my brakes and turned to stare at her and then the world slowed as the car started to skid.

I skidded for a long, long time, and the wheels must have been screaming but I didn't hear them. I was hurtling through a strange, silent world, lights flashing all around me. I felt the dull thud of metal on metal as the car skidded sideways, hit another car, hard metal folding easy as paper. The windscreen shattered like stars and the shiny shards fell like rain and kept falling, and the world looked like a kaleidoscope, pieces of light. Shadowy people running.

Then the noise started, sirens and screams and glass shattering. Somebody hauled me out of the car. There was a man with his hands on his head saying something about his fucking car and a shattered shop window with a mannequin in a blue sari leaning out through the hole. There were lots of people staring but I couldn't see Cal's mother.

Then it occurred to me that if she was here, he must be too, and this time the bastard was going to face me. I tried

46

to push through the crowd but someone held me back. I couldn't see him so I shouted: "What did you do it for? You stupid bastard. You stupid, stupid bastard."

I remembered all the things I'd never said to him. I put my head back and breathed. I could feel him in the hot wind. "You're my best friend," I shouted at the sky as a police officer grabbed my arms and flung me against a wall. "He was my best friend," I told him, and my face was wet. His mouth was moving but I couldn't hear the words.

I looked at the sky. Seabirds, swooped, pale as ghosts. I thought of my mother paused in a doorway. I thought of a thin arm stretched across a pillow.

"You do not need to say anything," he said, cuffing me. And I realised I did need to say something. But not to him.

And something breathed inside my head like air.

About the author:
Catrin Kean is a scriptwriter who has worked for film, radio and television. She was one of four writers awarded the Dennis Potter award in 2000, and her film *Gwyfyn* (S4C) won a Wales Bafta award for best drama. She has recently started writing fiction and her first short story, *Dust*, was published in the Riptide Journal number 8.

Billy and the Shaman

Ben Osborn

The foxes are screaming tonight. In between the pools of light, where the Shaman is hobbling, he makes a high lonesome barking sound in reply.

"Are you talking Fox?" says Billy to the Shaman.

"What does it sound like? Of course I bloody am," says the Shaman. His accent is nasal and North American but he has picked up a lot of English turns-of-phrase. "Hey," he squeaks in human, but to the foxes, "hey come back here, I'm not done talking to you."

"How did you learn to speak Fox?" says Billy, walking next to the Shaman. Billy is a very tall man, with long hair tied in a ponytail. His hair is the colour of sand and very nearly its texture. Like the Shaman, he wears all black.

"For chrissake," says the Shaman, "I speak Fox because sometimes I'm a fox. Will you shut up for a second?" he says, like he's interrupting himself, and then, clearly, to Billy, "no more stupid questions" – as if to prove that it's Billy he's annoyed with, and not his own self – then, very quiet, to the night or the foxes or something, he says, "I'm listening, I'm trying to listen…"

At 2pm the next day, Billy and the Shaman don't appear to have slept. They've got to the point where neither seems certain as to who is following whom – is Billy some protégé of the Shaman's, or is he studying the Shaman out of a more detached curiosity, journalistic, academic (though he is clearly neither journalist nor academic)? Or is the Shaman following Billy around? Perhaps it's some kind of curse on Billy? Or perhaps Billy looks after him and, for all his magical powers (which really aren't ever in doubt [so if you're doubting them please stop now]) perhaps he needs looking after in the Cartesian West, where body and soul aren't one and the same, where material and spirit are on different planes – the Cartesian West of Kings Cross, where he is hobbling, on the hunt – or perhaps the Shaman is studying Billy, trying to understand all the other strange people through Billy's example?

It is 2pm and it is July and a very hot July, a heatwave reaching its peak, and in the baking sun the little Shaman – he cannot be more than 5' 4", particularly apparent next to Billy who is like some mythical giant – his stick is only a little shorter than him, and as wizened as him, covered with strange symbols, runes and hieroglyphs and letters and words – in the baking sun the Shaman is, as always, all in black. His scalp is bare and a little blistered, gradually fading from pink to crimson in the direct sunlight. 2pm is when the monks from the local Hare Krishna temple park their van on York Way, by Kings Cross station, and ladle fat dollops of lentils and vegetables onto paper plates, food the colour of earth and trees and muddy streams, or beach-sand turmeric yellow, thick with brown smells, cumin and turmeric and sometimes flecks of old wilted coriander leaves, from great white plastic vats, from which they also give out thrown-out or soon-to-be-thrown-out food, packets of bread or bananas, tubs of cream cheese, lemons. The Shaman and Billy join the queue. Beside them is the man with the endless nose. Beside them the woman in the wheelchair. The oriental business man beside them. The polish builder. The art students. The penniless writers and composers living on the floors of their friends. The heartbroken and the openhearted. Tiny island in sea of

49

commuters, tourists, other elements of the flow. Tiny jutting rock in the stream.

The Hare Krishnas also have a little shop not far from there, on Caledonian Road, where they sell donated clothes and books and assorted assortments and odd oddments and bits of bobs and bob-bits. Outside the shop a girl called Kate is smoking and reading something. We smoke together. We talk, she very quickly, quite beautifully, like a beat poet or a raver on MDMA. I go into the store and buy a thick shirt that won't break, that will be good in all seasons, as I am planning a life of adventure, owning little, wanting less, going all places, always dreaming and reading and writing. Although this life is only in its planning stages she, I think, sees a little of it in me as we talk and smoke in the heat. In the shop, she and her manager drink Corona beer from plastic cups and dance as they work. The shirt costs maybe £2. I buy it and walk back toward Euston Road, walking southward I guess, and the manager runs after me yelling – "Hey! Hey, excuse me! Ex-cuse me!"

Oh God, I think. This life has broken me now. I must have taken something. An automatic habit picked up in supermarkets. Oh God, I've stolen from the Hare Krishnas, the harmless monks that feed the homeless and the penniless and the nevertheless and nonetheless oh yes the loneliness sneaks in, the soul as quantum singularity, a million conversations passing in front of my eardrums rendered pointless, a whole life metered and measured by a dance rhythm, an awkward two-step, out of time, rendering into clarity, oscillation of bright colour, sound turning into vision, space turning into time, one great gulp of oxygen and turn around and—

"You forgot something," she says, as I struggle to

50

forget anything that ever happened and went wrong, as I struggle to remember life has a flow, and can see only the rocks in the river, the way ripples run off them in endless diminishing-to-invisibility reflections of themselves, "I'm sorry?" I say as a question and—

"You forgot to get Kate's number," she says.

"Oh – I wasn't going to—" the sheen of calmness on me, one with all things, vestige and persona and idol of Great Spirit – "that would be a little rude, she's just trying to do her job, I don't want to—"

"Come get her number," insists the shopkeeper and I return and I get her number and for some time my head is full of Kate.

Between the Hare Krishna shop and the little Italian shop called 'Continental Supplies' or something, which the owner opens in 1964, when he arrives from Italy and purchases a machine that slices bread, cheese and meat and he sells bread cheese and meat, slicing it using the machine, and he lights the place almost only with sunlight and there's always other old Italian men in there, only breaking their half-sleep by the counter to launch into violently animated conversations in Italian – between the two stores but on the other side of the road, this is where I first spot Billy and the Shaman. Billy is reading outside the supermarket, reading a thin book or perhaps a pamphlet, and the Shaman emerges out of the scant shadows of late afternoon heatwave London, his staff thrown out madly in front of him, striking the tarmac, grunting to Billy, high nasal North American whine, "Hey, I'm not done talking to you" – like Billy was a fox.

I wanted to ask Billy how he ended up with the Shaman; did one choose the other, was their friendship force-fed, was it a case of mutually assured destruction? I wanted to ask Billy: is your name really Billy? Because you look so much like a Billy. It seems too much of a coincidence that it would really be your name.

But I never even caught his name really. I was distracted by the nutshells that fell from the trees around Euston Square, the way the wind left them on the windowsills of the surrounding buildings, the way that they resembled the outgrown exoskeletons of arthropods.

About the author:

Ben Osborn is a writer, songwriter and composer. As musical director of Fellswoop Theatre his productions have won the Cameron Macintosh Award, the Wildfire Award and the Methuen Emerging Artists Award. His stories have appeared in various publications and his libretto *On false perspective* was set to music by composer Josephine Stephenson and performed this year.

benosborn.blogspot.com

Cat in the Snow

L F Roth

There was the miscarriage; there was the cat. She connected the two. Who wouldn't? But very soon doubt entered her mind. Was life ever that simple? If it was, why at this point? Why not the first time around? And why a cat? In some ways she shared Robert's opinion. "Dogs," he had said on one occasion, eyeing a Rottweiler that was charging down the street, a broken chain clattering behind it. "Dogs are useful." A hair's breadth ahead a cat squeezed under a fence. Phew! Dee shivered at the memory. "They'll fetch and carry. They'll protect you. They'll die for you. A cat will only save its own skin. What good is that?" Now, she wouldn't stand by to see a cat butchered by a Rottweiler, but other than that she agreed. Cats were no more special than, say, crickets.

So when she first caught sight of it out back, beside the small greenhouse, she noted its presence but that was all. Even that took some doing; she could barely make out the shape in the snow, not primarily because of its spectral whiteness, but because it kept so still. It took an effort to trace the opaque eyes, which neither blinked nor shifted position, and the pale pink nose, held rigidly still. She had no idea what possessed her to crouch down, once she was convinced those were eyes, that was a nose, and call out, but no matter: the cat didn't respond. To Dee, that was a mark of past abuse, if not from Rottweilers then from some human beast. Perhaps to make up for it she got a small bowl and a couple of tins of cat food from the pet shop the same afternoon. She placed the bowl in the spot where the cat had been and lingered for a while. The cat had left no imprint in the snow.

Inside Robert's voice greeted her.

"Did you go out at all today?"

"Briefly," she told him.

"You know what the doctor recommended."

"I know," she said. "Well, it was less than that."

"Why don't you try swimming?"

But she shook her head. She didn't feel at home in her body just yet. She wasn't sure how far she could trust it.

The food was still there in the morning. She picked up the bowl. "Here, cat," she called, rattling the frozen bits in case the cat was within hearing. A name would simplify things. Kitty? Molly? Snowy? Of course, whatever common name she chose might well be tainted. The gender posed another problem. Should it be male or female or, given the times, both? Female, probably, since the cat appeared to have been abused. Dee played with variations of her own name. Audrey? Deirdre? Delia? She tested them one at a time. Both whispered and spoken aloud she found the sound of Delia the most appealing. The movement of her tongue was pleasingly smooth, as it shifted gently from the ridge behind her upper teeth to the area a little further back before lowering itself to let the final vowel through. De-li-a. Spoken too fast, it became a sloppy De-l-ya. No cat would want that. "De-li-a," she called. "Here, De-li-a." No shadow moved across the snow.

To occupy herself she carefully inscribed the name on the side of the bowl, pausing after each stroke, worried that the marker would slip on the glossy surface. She didn't dare try curlicues and so the result was a lot less smooth than she would have liked it, especially when it came to the three rounded letters: they wound up much too angular. Worse, all five of them seemed bristly. She had used permanent black ink, but turpentine might remove it all the same. Would a renewed effort pay off? She thought not. She refilled the bowl and put it back outside. She would wait for the cat's reaction.

But reaction there was none, if you didn't regard the disappearance of the food as one. By late afternoon every last scrap was gone. The name had not put the cat off, nor had the smell of ink. Bending down to bring the bowl inside, Dee saw a bird hiding in the bushes and shooed it away. "It's cat food," she said. She immediately regretted the action. What if the cat had left a morsel as bait, preferring wild game to factory food, and had been ready to spring on the bird the moment Dee opened the door? She glanced at the empty bowl. Birdseed was the answer. She could make another trip to the shop. She tried to imagine a brief exchange with Robert on the topic. "Today I went for a walk," she could say. "I was clean out of bird food." But she was unable to think of a reply. There were so many things they'd never talked about, bird food being just one. They'd never had any, had they? But the bird would hardly come back in a hurry – it would be dark shortly. In any case, the cat may very well have eaten all the food herself, not caring in the least for birds. Dee pictured her with a limp bird in her claws and saw her gag on blood-stained down and bits of bone. She erased the image. That wasn't the sort of cat she'd want in her garden.

Over the next few days, she filled the bowl morning and night, as if the initial feed had made the cat her responsibility. It called for persistence: she hadn't seen the animal after that first time, even though she'd been getting up earlier than she used to, before it was properly light – cats hunted at dawn and dusk, didn't they? Having the bedroom to herself helped. That only used to happen when Robert was away at a conference or for a job interview.

Mostly he'd let her know both when and where, and maybe even why, but at times it had slipped his mind. Or hers? On those occasions she had always worried, unable to appreciate the space his absence afforded her. Now she no longer had that worry.

Delia had found a space for herself too, Dee discovered late one day, but again she had to look twice to be quite sure she wasn't seeing things. Legs tucked in under her, the cat was one almost with the white bonnet of her neighbour's car where it stood in the driveway, the engine presumably giving off heat after a recent run. In the low sunlight, it was the translucent blue of her eyes that gave the cat away. "You'd be better off on my side of the hedge," Dee warned her. Judging from what little she had seen of people in the area, they weren't likely to throw their doors open to strangers, let alone cats. Her neighbour's leaf blower would make short work of her. Not that Dee differed greatly in terms of hospitality; she wouldn't want a cat in the house herself. They marked their territory, indoors and out. They made scratch marks. They tore things. A life without a cat suited her fine.

But what good was her resolve? She had no more than confirmed it when the cat made her way in.

"How was your day?" she heard Robert ask.

"No different," she told him.

"You have to eat. The doc…"

"I know." She shouldn't cut him short. "I will," she said, out of habit, to oblige, as if it would make the least difference. Why so solicitous? "It was none of my doing," he had insisted. "You brought it on yourself." She went into the kitchen and opened the door to the fridge. There were eggs. She didn't want eggs. There were sausages. How long had she had those? They would be off, wouldn't they? There was very little else. She disposed of the sausages and made herself a cheese omelette. Then, frying pan in hand, she turned around and there, perched on the shelf that held her two cookery books and the tea caddy, was the cat. She returned the pan to the cooker with a clank and spun around to face her – but too late. The cat was gone, having left not even a draught behind. The cookery books stood undisturbed the way they had for months. The metal tea caddy bore no smudge mark that could be attributed to a cat's nose. Dee stared in disbelief.

"Eat," she told herself. She transferred the omelette to her plate and moved the plate so she would face the doorway rather than the window. "Eat. Then search all the rooms."

She did, but saw no sign of a cat – she even crossed the threshold of what had again become the spare room, a space she knew not how to fill. How had it got in? And, more to the point, where had it gone? Had she forgotten to pull the door to? Had it slunk in alongside her? Had someone let it in? Robert? Had he, without her knowledge, had a new key made? Having nothing but questions she inspected the ground-floor windows one more time, but everything was as it should be.

To ease the tension that had built up, she made herself a cup of tea and took it into the sitting room, where her chair welcomed her back. Weeks must have passed. The cramps. The bleeding. The uncertainty. Here, too, across the room, were shelves, half emptied out, which could have held a whole litter of cats – she had read of old women whose cats came to fill the entire house. Out of the corner of her eye she caught sight of a small urn, a wedding gift she hadn't seen for years. Had it not shattered? She couldn't recall mending it. She blinked and it was gone. Once spring arrived she would pick vases of flowers to bring the room to life.

She closed her eyes. Before her was a path deep in the woods, with sunlight filtering through light green leaves, a carpet of wood anemones – cowslips would come later, wouldn't they? – and butterflies dancing in the air. Violets? A cat – Delia – was coming towards her, with two, no three kittens in tow, one black, one white, one tiger striped, sniffing the flowers, swiping at the butterflies. There must have been a father, but he was gone, missed by no one. Why should they care? Delia would do for them.

Dee opened her eyes to blot out the picture and heard Delia hiss.

She would have been smaller even than those kittens not so long ago.

"I could have done for you," she said.

But why waste sentiment on a cat that came and went as it pleased?

Still, conscientiously, she put out food morning and night and Delia, equally conscientiously, licked the bowl clean. At one time winter loosened its grip for a few days and Dee left the door ajar, to air the house. But air was all that entered. From inside she perceived a dull thud as snow slid off the roof. Another followed. She stepped out to size up the mounds, checking that there was no overhang above the door. Some of her neighbours' roofs were much steeper than hers. Could they prove hazardous to the cat? They might, she decided, if there were icicles as well as snow. But what could she do? The cat just had to take its chances. Rottweilers. Leaf blowers. Ice. That the food disappeared proved that she was as yet unharmed.

Then one day winter was truly on the wane. The sun rose earlier and as Dee placed her breakfast cup on the arm of her chair in the sitting room, its rays played on the wall across from her. "Here, pet," she whispered, and there was the cat on one of the shelves, her coat electrified. Dee caressed her with her eyes, exulting in her perfect shape, her colouring, her poise, noting the exquisite grace with which each action was performed, her ears turning almost imperceptibly at the least sound, the pink inside changing in aspect as the light hit it at a different angle, her whiskers floating on the air in perfect symmetry, the muscles of her body playing as she stretched, pushing her front paws out, pulling them in, her tail one moment a sorcerer's wand, the next a bullwhip. However slight the variations were, Dee was transfixed. She could have watched the cat all day.

"My Delia," she said. She was aware of a faint miaow in reply and reached out. But there was no one there.

No one there. No one anywhere.

She closed her eyes but doing so shut nothing out, brought nothing into view.

That night she went to bed without having gone near the back garden. Let the cat fend for itself, she decided. Let it catch birds – there were more of them each day. Who cares if it chokes on the feathers? Let it live off what nature has to offer. Let it try its luck with the neighbours.

She slept badly, hearing the cat in her sleep. Near dawn she all but gave up: the cat, she felt, was in the bedroom with her, moving about restlessly. She examined the top of the wardrobe, the dresser, the space under the chair that was in part covered by her clothes, but saw no sign of her. Again she tried to bring on sleep, taking slow breaths, but sleep wouldn't come. Finally, in the early morning, she must have dozed off.

What woke her was the cat's slow progress from the foot end of the bed, each movement so minimal that it assured her she was dreaming. It crept along her legs. Gently she drew back the cover to make room for it beside her; it curled up on her stomach and started purring. Warmth spread through her like an infusion of new blood. Their breathing synchronized. There was no outside world.

And then the outside world intruded, as Dee sought the softness of Delia's coat. What her hand came to rest on was no cat. There were no pointed ears, no whiskers, no tail. What her fingers caressed wasn't fur but skin, cold to the touch. "No," she whispered. A shiver ran through her. "Don't. Please don't. I never wanted you. I never did." Her words hung in the air. But the claim, no more true than the reverse, brought only pain.

About the author:
L. F. Roth: No tinker, tailor, soldier, sailor, though a full CV could list a number of other occupations – but then, who cares? What matters is the fiction. A writerly CV would have fewer entries, among them short stories published by Biscuit (2011), Segora (web, 2012) and Earlyworks Press (2012, 2013, 2014).

Daylight Saving

Marc Owen Jones

Andrew's reading the paper on the sofa and Debbie's on the computer. Classic FM murmurs in the background and spring rain patters silently on the floor to ceiling windows. It's an overcast mid-morning but the automatic lighting warms the room. From the end of the walled-in garden they're a human exhibit for small mammals and brave burglars.

"Have you seen this?" she says.

"Seen what, dear?"

"This email from Ted."

"What's he got to say for himself?"

"Cheeky bastard."

Andrew closes the cover on his tablet, stands up and wanders over to his wife. He rests his hands gently on her shoulders and peers at the screen. He is momentarily reminded of the miracle of laser eye surgery.

"Do you remember the other day, when I hadn't quite heard what you'd said and you sniped at me and I snarled back?"

"You didn't snarl, pumpkin, you purred," he says and leans forward to plant a kiss on her cheek.

"Quite," she strokes the side of his face before continuing, "but these are Ted's words." She shifts her head sideways so that he can get a better view. "Anyway, the station's saying there was a positive blip in the ratings after that. More people stayed on during the ad break and for a few hours we were trending, whatever that means. They're saying we should do more stuff like that."

"More stuff like what?"

"You know, contentious, argumentative."

"But we're Mr and Mrs Happily Married."

"They're saying that people want to see us disagreeing once in a while."

"I'm not sure I can do that."

"It looks like we're going to have to try."

"Or what? They'll cancel us? Come off it Debbie, *Daylight Saving*'s our segment. We own it. They're hardly going to pull it just because we look too happy."

"I know, darling, but I think we might have to meet them half way on this. Ted's pretty blunt." She tilts her head and Andrew lowers his head. They kiss and it feels as soft and sensual as it did when they'd first met.

They stare at each other in the dressing room mirror, breathless and exhilarated. Andrew is laughing so much that tears streak his makeup. He wipes them away with the back of his hand and his face turns two-tone. This makes him laugh harder and Debbie joins in.

"I want you," she says.

"Now?" Andrew looks at his wife with renewed lust. Their sex life is good, but for more years than he can remember it has been a weekly fixture in his diary, like squash.

"Now," she confirms and Andrew jumps up, but before he can twist the lock on the door, it opens.

"Perfect," Ted says. He's a small man with a big voice. People who haven't seen him assume he's tall and handsome. In the flesh he disappoints; so nondescript that people look beyond him to the person they presume must be just behind. Andrew pulls up short and turns his reach into a stretch. "Are you okay?" Ted says.

"We're fine, now sod off, I want to get changed," she says.

Ted widens his grin, "just one thing before I leave you

gorgeous people to your own devices. Let's get some social media pumping. Andrew, put out a tweet saying 'I'm mightily pissed off' and Debbie, update your Facebook with 'serves him right'." He looks at both of them in turn, waiting for their agreement. They nod and he leaves with, "Good work, darlings, keep it up," trailing behind him.

Andrew locks the door and looks at his wife.

"Tweet first, then sex," she says.

Each morning they find something to disagree about. They bicker and press buttons that they had thought had been smoothed to invisibility by the consideration of marriage. The disagreements take on a life of their own as the public use their example to question their own relationships. Each tweet or post is endlessly debated and too many to read answer back, in progressively shorter and more caustic language. Andrew chooses not to read them. Debbie pretends not to care.

"This morning we are delighted to welcome the inventor of this remarkable device that will save you money every day." Debbie holds up a sponge to camera; it's ten inches long and banana yellow. The focus is tight and her expression doesn't change. She smiles with the primness of Miss Brodie. "Its revolutionary design not only absorbs moisture with fifty percent more efficiency than a normal sponge, but it also lasts more than three times longer."

The camera pulls back. Debbie is sitting at one end of the sofa and Andrew is at the other. A bespectacled forty-year-old in a cheap suit, button down shirt and polyester tie sits uncomfortably between them. "Eric Naughty…"

"I think you'll find that's pronounced 'knock-tee'," Andrew interrupts. "Although looking at his sponge you might have been right the first time." Suppressed snorts

63

are heard off camera and Mr Naughtie blushes.

"I apologise for my husband who appears to have regressed to childhood this morning," she says and flashes a look of such contempt that Eric withers between them.

"You are quite right, Debbie dear. Now tell me Mr Naughtie, what was on your mind when you engineered the shape of your marvellous new sponge?"

They both smile at Eric who looks from one to the other. "I, err, wasn't thinking about shape per se. It is the molecular composition of sponge that dictates the optimum shape."

"Unfortunately phallic though, don't you think?" Andrew says.

"Why bright yellow?" Debbie interrupts.

"The colour wasn't necessarily a consideration."

"The sponge-bob fallacy," Andrew giggles.

"Grow up Andrew. I'm sorry Mr Naughtie, please continue."

Debbie holds onto one end of the sponge and Eric the other. Andrew is chocking back hysterics and off-camera the laughs are less restrained. Debbie asks questions with a face growing harder by the moment. Her jaw muscles contract and steel flints her brown eyes.

"Thank you, Mr Naughtie." The camera pulls in, "Tomorrow we will be meeting the brains behind the latest must-have scented candle and asking our experts 'what's so special about compound interest?' So, until tomorrow, see what you can save today."

The camera pans to Andrew who waves goodbye, unable to speak.

"Andrew, that was unacceptable," Debbie says as soon as the floor manager has confirmed that they're off air.

"It's a cock."

"It's a sponge. We're broadcasting to a mid-morning

audience of housewives and pensioners; they do not want to experience your juvenile behaviour."

"Oh come on Debbie, it was funny." He looks around the crew for confirmation. They all look down to the floor as Debbie storms off. "Whoops," he says to no one. And that is the word he types into Twitter with a picture of the phallic sponge. It's the most favourited and retweeted post he's ever done and his followers leap twenty percent to breach the hundred thousand mark. The dressing room door is locked and so he wipes off his make-up in the guests' area and drives home alone.

Debbie hires a social media manager and takes him to lunch at Quaglino's. He is in his late twenties, clean shaven and wide eyed; a younger and more athletic version of Andrew, Debbie thinks. She is attracted by his knowledge and flattered by his attention. She loves the fact that she has to tell him that she's a married woman as they wait for separate taxis in the late afternoon. Her Facebook likes leap-frog Andrew's followers within days.

"Are you and Mum not talking?" Sam, their nineteen-year-old son, is murdering hookers on the large flat screen in his bedroom.

"We're fine," Andrew says as he sits down next to Sam and picks up the other controller.

"Whatever."

"We are," he reiterates with less conviction. He watches as his character, the spit of Bruce Willis, is pummelled to death without speaking. "Have you got any grass?"

"I don't…"

"You do, I can smell it. Have you got any? I'll pay you back." Andrew looks at his son who stops playing and returns his gaze.

"Top drawer," he shrugs. "Do you want me to roll you one?"

"Please." Andrew watches as his son rolls the perfect spliff with practised efficiency. He's far better than he had ever been he thinks, and he wonders whether he should be concerned. Sam passes him the joint. "Thanks," he mutters and leaves him to his game.

The motion sensor lights have already brightened the garden before Andrew walks down to the office. It must be next door's cat he thinks and mentally files the need to have the lights recalibrated. He stands inside the office looking out onto the lawn until the night shuts out sight. He pulls a beer out of the fridge, turns on Pink Floyd and lights up. The first drag makes him cough, the second makes him appreciate the strength, the third makes him realise that he's never had anything quite like this before. He doesn't remember how many tokes he takes after that. What he does remember is that drugs are a mood accelerator and can't change his underlying temperament; when he was happy he became ecstatic and when he was sad he became suicidal. Now, he finds himself sinking into a depression so profound that he sincerely believes that his marriage is irreparable. He knows with absolute certainty that Debbie is sleeping with someone else, that the affair is more than sex and that he is as forgotten as last week's guests in her affections. There is no longer any pretence in the antipathy they feel for each other and they have never been more popular. He cries and it feels more heartfelt than any emotion he has ever experienced.

Dinner suited in the afternoon they walk up the red carpet at the TV Awards. Debbie reaches for his hand but he pulls away, pocketing it before their fingers touch. "Not now," she hisses. Andrew ignores her, strides up the carpet into the theatre and takes his seat without looking back. She pretends a journalist has called her over and stops to chat. She shrugs and smiles as if to say 'husbands', but is seething inside. She is astonished, when looking through the pictures online, that her anger didn't show. For the first time they cross legs away from each other.

They sell their stories to different tabloids; each trying to out-do the other with compound hurt feelings and remorse. They turn down talk shows and events; there are now too many to accept. Andrew chats up the wardrobe assistant but cannot bring himself to cheat. Debbie sleeps with her social Adonis out of spite, positive that he had. Sam moves out and would have said 'a plague on both your houses' if either of his parents had noticed him packing up his car. Andrew changes the light bulbs in the garden but they still come on at odd times, startling the night.

Ted calls round. In any other circumstance this would be a red letter day; he has never before been known to venture out to the wilds of Barnes without an escort. Andrew and Debbie stand on opposite sides of the sitting room and Ted drums his foot awkwardly between them.

"Drink?" Andrew says.

"Gin and Tonic, thanks."

"I'll have the same," Debbie says.

"Whatever."

"Do you see what I have to put up with? It's like living with a teenager."

"Well at least I'm not screwing one."

"How many times do I have to tell you?"

"Nothing you say will make it any less true."

"Andrew, Debbie, please," Ted begs.

Andrew makes drinks and Debbie sits down, waving at

Ted to join her. He carries the drinks over, hands Ted his and places Debbie's on the table beside her, just out of reach. He sits down opposite the two of them and nurses a scotch.

"This has gone too far. The network is getting worried and, frankly, so am I. This was supposed to be some light banter to spice up the show, not all out war." He talks patiently but with an edge, like a headmaster admonishing two unruly pupils. "You've both raised your profiles to unprecedented heights, it's now time to consolidate your celebrity and join forces again."

Andrew stands up and marches to the French windows. He opens the door and stands on the terrace looking out onto his illuminated garden. "These bloody lights are driving me nuts," he says to Ted. "I've had the men out twice and they still come on at all times of night."

"It's next door's cat. Just close the door, Ted was talking."

Andrew debates the futility of embarking on another argument and decides not to, in deference to Ted.

"Anyway," Ted continues, "I've been in touch with *HELLO!* and they want to do a spread on the two of you; at home, loved up and happy. They're offering a half a million. What do I say?"

"Say yes," Andrew and Debbie say together.

"Leave him and leave the show. With your interaction stats you can get your own show in the States." Social Media Mike is naked on the bed staring at the ceiling. Debbie has her head in his lap and can't speak. *HELLO!* is open beside them, her home unrecognisable, their smiles airbrushed into existence. She can't for the life of her remember why she had agreed to the final sentence:

68

Debbie and Andrew are looking forward to renewing their wedding vows whilst on holiday in Barbados next month.

Andrew has taken over Sam's room. Fag ends overflow the ashtray and coke residue dusts the table top. He's lost within the game with every sense heightened; dealing, driving and killing to a new high score. The curtains are closed and so he doesn't see the motion sensor lights come on. The volume is so high that he doesn't hear the French doors open. Desperate for the loo he presses pause and the residual echo of bangs and shouts vibrate in his eardrums. He doesn't see the intruder until it's too late. The baseball bat smashes into his skull and he collapses on the landing. His eyes register dark trousers and trainers. He hears nothing. He feels nothing. He dies.

Debbie models her grief on Jackie Kennedy; proud, dignified and unbearably sad. But there is nothing she can do to prevent the trolling. Andrew's drug habit comes under scrutiny and commentators can't help but link his use to sadness. Where she was at the time (in the arms of a man young enough to be her son) is, in the eyes of the media, reason enough for that sorrow: Andrew was killed defending his home whilst she was out destroying their family. Her fame amplifies the condemnation and nobody wants to know her now; not the network, not America, not Social Media Mike and not Sam.

About the author:
Marc Owen Jones is currently writing a novel and a linked collection of short stories. His story *The Murder of Crows* was recently published by Unthank Books in Unthology 4 and *Gameshow* was longlisted for the Fish Prize 2014. Marc lives in a small village just outside Norwich and works in the holiday industry. He can be found at www.marcowenjones.com and can be followed on twitter @marcgjones.

How It Begins

Sarah Evans

The bell rings early morning and when I open the door I see the flower. A single rose, a white one. Only for a second do I falter.

I do not scour the surroundings with rabbit-twitching eyes.

I do not go rushing out, engaging in a futile game of seek and hide.

I simply crouch to pick it up before retreating. Door closed, I press my spine against the wall and I tighten every muscle to be strong. Then something entirely different washes over and I start to laugh, swept through by the headiness of relief. It's happened. The wait is over.

It is day one and I need to plan.

It always starts with flowers, with a colourless, fragrance-free rose. I place it in a large vase; after all, the flower is blameless. Each day I open the door with false verve and a numb sense of inevitability. Each day, the roses accumulate, following the spectrum from pastel-pale pink through to shocking.

On day seven, the rose is dead, its petals brittle and smelling sweetly of decay. But it retains its pigment – carmine – the colour of dried blood.

I do not go to the police, pleading harassment. I do not cower and hide and refuse to answer the door. I do not visit my doctor and ask for pills to dissolve away the fretting and allow sleep.

I have learned by now, none of these things help.

It is day eight. Returning home, I find a card sitting on my doormat. There is no stamp or postmark. The envelope is white and the handwriting – *dearest Liz* – is as familiar as my own.

Inside is a Valentine's card, even though it's April. An embossed heart springs out from the surface, its texture fuzzy and soft. The printed verse comes with curlicues and florid declarations of devotion. It is headed *my darling girl* and ends with, *all my love, always, your Drusilla.*

Each day another card awaits me when I get back from somewhere, a sequence of pink tinted envelopes. The phrasing varies, the exact words, but always expressing the same things. She loves me. She knows that I love her. She dreams of the day we will be together.

Soon, my love, she writes, *very soon.*

She is full of understanding.

I know why you have done the things you've done, she says. *I forgive you.*

And all the while, I go about my daily purpose, keeping outward appearances normal. I do not look behind me on the street or keep the curtains closed. I do not wear sunglasses, or slink into the shadows.

I start to wind down my life, as unobtrusively as possible. The practicalities have become easier, now I am unencumbered by trappings of permanency.

I give notice on the house and pay off the remaining rent. I reduce possessions down to what I can easily carry. There is no one in particular I need to say farewell to.

This is my life and these are the things I have learned to do.

Day fourteen, I return from grocery shopping in which I have acquired wine and eggs, gathering my requirements haphazardly, making seemingly random purchases on different days. I have no idea how much of my daily pattern – work, supermarket, evenings in front of the TV – she watches. I have not so much as glimpsed her. She is very good at her game.

Today the envelope is red, the colour of passion and of fury. Of both love and hate.

I make tea I have no desire to drink. My laptop updates me on news headlines and the weather. I ready myself to go out again, this time to the garden centre, and I think how later I will cut back and bag up the nettles in the backyard to justify my purchase.

First, I open the card. The verse is penned by her this time. She talks about destiny, moonbeams and watching sunsets hand in hand. Each line glistens in haemoglobin ink.

You can't run from this forever, she writes.

My lips press tight. She's right. This time, I am not going to run, at least not in the usual way.

This time, there will be an end.

Day fifteen and I ring in sick. I do not inform work that I will not be back; in the come-and-go space of the call centre, my departure will be quickly closed over, as if I'd never been there. I wonder if she will find this odd, the alteration to my routine, but I try not to dwell on it as I busy myself in the kitchen, humming along to radio songs of love and heartbreak. I measure flour, sugar, margarine; I beat in eggs, vanilla, spice. I spoon the mixture into paper cases and place the tray in the preheated oven.

I mix butter, icing sugar, water and add drops of cochineal. I remember gifts, boxes of half-eaten, heart-shaped chocolates, providing evidence of the sweetness of her tooth.

In the bedroom, I dig out the pills I have not taken for some time. I unwrap my newly purchased pestle and mortar and I grind a number of the tablets down, pummelling and twisting, until my wrist aches and the pills are fine as powdered sugar. The air fills with the sickly-sweet scent of baking. I remove the golden-brown cakes and leave them on the side.

The phone rings and it does not startle me. I do not ask myself how she got hold of my ex-directory number; I have come to accept her complete genius in these things. I wipe my hands and proceed over at my own pace. I pick up and listen to the pause of silence.

"I knew you'd ring," I say.

Time carries me forward. The cakes are cool to touch and on one of them I inscribe a pink heart in frosted buttercream. The effect is far from perfect, but it's a close enough approximation and isn't love supposed to be blind. On a second cake, I enact the same heart, then deliberately smudge the icing.

Clumsy me. But you must have the better one. I cannot quite picture the woman who might say those things.

I pack bags and leave them in the hallway. I tidy my hair back in a rubber band. I tuck the items I require deep in my shoulder bag and place the two cakes in a Tupperware box, which goes into a carrier bag along with the bottle of sweet pink fizzy wine, the sort I never, ever drink.

I leave the house and follow the route I have looked up and memorised, walking to a regular rhythm. It isn't far and I wonder how long she has lived here, both of us breathing the same air, both greeted daily by the curve of green hills rising above the grey-slate roofs of the town. She had wanted to come to me and I had to be quite forceful in insisting, "No, no. It's my turn to come to yours."

I am extraordinarily calm and it takes me by surprise, the silent pumping of my heart, the automatic reflex of my lungs. My body signals no distress, as if even my deepest psyche is convinced there is no other way.

I linger on the corner. She will be waiting and I wonder what it is that she expects. She has every reason to suppose I will not show, yet *reason* has never applied to any of this. At one minute to the appointed hour, I continue onwards. I fix my smile and press the intercom button. The door opens immediately.

She is shorter than I remember and heavier. Her hair is unnatural blond and her lips scarlet. She is exceptionally plain, a pig nose snubbing upwards from a doughy face.

Time hesitates and falters. It is rare that we scrutinise each other openly, and I wonder whether just doing this might snap both of us out of the coming sequence of events.

Only for a second do I think that.

"Well," I say, all falsely jolly. "Can I come in?"

I watch for suspicion, because the one thing she is not is stupid.

"I knew you'd come," she says. Her smile is almost shy.

"I said I would."

I follow her along a dimly lit, dank corridor.

Her studio flat is grim in all the ways I had not stopped to imagine. A poorly fitted kitchenette, with double electric ring. A sagging sofa. A three-quarter bed swamped by a beige duvet. The air smells of mildew and unwashed socks. The carpet is worn to threads. The only splash of colour comes from the pin-board above the bed with its collage of photos and I know without looking what they are of.

I lift up the bottle of wine. "To celebrate," I say.

I keep my eyes on her as I make for the sofa. I take off

my floppy hat and gloves, because not doing so might seem strange. "Hope you don't mind me making myself at home." The door closes. The only window is above the sink and too narrow for easy exit. She carries more weight than me, has home-field advantage and who knows what she means by *destiny*. It comes to me for the thousandth time that I am introducing a new and precarious element to all this and I have no idea how it might affect her, what tipping point I might trigger in her disturbed mind.

Requitement has never been part of how this goes.

She is strangely silent, this woman who over the years has bombarded me with great outpourings of words. By letter. Phone. Tape. Occasionally face to face.

Perhaps she is waiting for the trick, for me to cut the simpering smile and begin to state in clear, bold terms what exactly I do not – and will never – feel. For me to plead with her to leave me alone. The way I have done before.

Never argue delusions with the delusional. It's the first rule of psychiatry and deeply difficult to stick to.

I plunge on recklessly, throwing myself into the game that is not my own. "D'you have glasses?" I say. "And plates?"

She hovers above me, gazing at the dun-coloured swirls beneath my feet. "Shall I help?" I spring up and back, catching the scent of stale sweat mingling with cheap perfume, of bad breath and spearmint. I can see the grey of her hair at its roots and the leakage of lipstick into the capillary lines fanning out from her lips.

"No, no," she says. "You sit down."

She fumbles in the cupboard and produces two cloudy tumblers, and picnic plates decorated with hearts and flowers. Her movements are odd somehow, as if miscalculating the space around her. I watch intently, alert to her every move. She sits beside me. I open the wine and pour, clumsily, so the bubbles froth up and nearly over.

"Here." I pick up one glass and gesture the other, careful to touch as few surfaces as possible. The glasses clunk together; we both sip. "Isn't this lovely," I say.

Her lower lip trembles. "Drusilla," I say, as gently as I am able.

"It's just…" Her voice wavers and she looks up, eyes brimful of tears. "It's just I've waited so long for this, my darling."

"I know."

"You haven't always been kind."

"No. But you understand the reasons don't you?"

"I do, I do."

"And now we'll always be together."

"Always." She says it like a sigh and looks like she might make a move towards me. I twist away as smoothly as possible, turning to pick up the Tupperware.

"I made some special cakes," I say and open the box.

"They look beautiful." Her eyes are wide and trusting, melting puppy-dog eyes.

"And hopefully delicious." I take mine then thrust the box towards her. It seems impossible she won't see through this whole charade, but I'm in too deep to do anything other than continue bluffing my way. "At least I hope so." I take a big bite. My mouth is dry and it feels like I'm chewing on syrup-saturated cardboard.

She picks up the cake and toys with the paper.

Eat the damned thing!

"I made them specially," I say. "For our special day." Like the buttercream, I am laying this on thick as I can.

"I know. I know. And they're beautiful it's just…"

My smile aches. *For fuck's sake.* "I made them specially."

76

"I just feel so… so… I don't know if I can…" She starts to cry, great snivelling sobs; it is not a pretty sight.

I wrestle down my revulsion and inch towards her, close enough that my arm can stretch out over her shoulders. I smell her anew. I feel her body warmth through the slimy texture of her floral blouse. I am close enough to see the pores on her nose and the individual whiskers on her chin.

"Hey," I say. "None of that. Let's drink the wine and eat the cake to celebrate."

"To celebrate our love."

"Yes. Our love."

She sniffs up loudly. Her hand gropes my knee. It takes every inch of self-restraint not to shove her away. I eat more cake.

"Now you," I say through my full mouth. "I'll be disappointed if you don't eat my cake." I am aiming for a loving, teasing tone.

Come on, you bitch, come on.

Then she smiles. A stomach-churning, cats-got-the-cream smile, revealing the gap in her front teeth. "I knew," she says. "I always knew."

"You did."

She lifts the cake to her mouth. She bites, chews and swallows. I watch for the contortion on her face, the detection of not-quite rightness, for the bitter realisation to show through. "It's wonderful," she says.

"Really?"

"Really."

"Only I'm not sure I'm that great a cook."

"Oh you are. You are. Everything about you is wonderful." And to prove it she eats every last crumb.

It is a different sort of waiting now, the waiting when you know the end is very close and that certain further

77

things will be required and then it will be over.

One last push.

I drink more of the wine in a play for time and refill the glasses. "We need to finish this too." It tastes sour after the sugar shock of the cake. "Our celebration champagne."

I keep up the chattering nonsense, picking up my lines from all those cards. I endure the close-up tang and clammy warmth of her and when I judge the moment right, I yawn.

"Sorry!" I exclaim. "Only I couldn't sleep last night, I was so excited. I knew you'd ring today."

She beams at me, a little girl smile, and I remind myself how there is absolutely nothing innocent about her. "I knew you'd know."

"Our special connection." I yawn again. And this time she mimics it back.

Please may that mean what I need it to.

"I'm tired too," she says.

"Well..." I'm all jolly hockey-sticks again. *How can she not see through this?* "Maybe the two of us are going to need an early night."

Her eyes cast away. I wonder if she has ever in her entire life had sex. Her letters and calls have always been thankfully vague and I have no idea what precisely her fantasies consist of. Whether like some old-time romantic film, her imagination stops with the fade-out and the swelling orchestra. Or whether she enacts the details.

I feel sick. I stand up, and my body sways; too much alcohol on an empty stomach. I reach down, my outstretched fingers seeking hers. Her palm is sticky. She pulls my wrist to her lips and it makes me think of slugs, of leeches, and I badly want to scream.

She follows me, dog-obedient, to the bed.

78

"What an amazing collage," I say, scrabbling for a second's postponement. "Just look at how much effort you put in."

"I did it for you." Her cheeks are aglow with happiness and love, looking every bit the attention-hungry ten-year-old awarded a gold star by her favourite teacher.

I allow her this moment. I force myself to look at the photos she has taken over the years and had printed in bright Kodak colour, most of them a little fuzzy, taken from a distance, and all of them of me. In between are mementos from my life. Ticket stubs for films and plays and exhibitions, back in the days when I used to go out to things. Post-it notes covered in my messy scrawl and others on which she has written addresses and phone numbers from each of my attempts at escape. A till receipt for that fizzy wine and a sandwich wrapper from my Friday lunch. I recognise a Valentine's card I gave so many years ago, pinned up so that it gapes open and I can see how she has tippexed out the word *Mike* and replaced it with her own.

I gaze hard at my words – *love always* – and gather my strength.

"It's amazing," I repeat. "I just..." My eyes dip coyly downwards. "I just need to use the bathroom. Why don't you lie down?"

I bolt the bathroom door behind me. For the first time my heart is battering furious and hard. My stomach convulses and I taste vanilla mixed with bile. I run the scaled-up tap to scalding hot and wash and wash her touch away. I splash cold water on my face, breathe in the scent of mould and wait for my body to slip back into icy calm.

I am so very nearly there.

She is lying on the bed, still fully clothed, one hand flung back against the pillow, her eyes closed and her mouth gaping moistly open. I wish this was all there is to it, but sleeping-pills alone are far too unreliable and I need to make absolutely sure.

I retrieve my gloves and bag from the sofa. I extract the heavy-duty garden sack with its toughened drawstring top. I remember, once, stealing myself against the skin-crawling repugnance of picking up a dead pigeon from our lawn, the lawn that existed in a different life, back when Mike and I were happily in love, the two of us talking about our future.

I place one knee on the bed and lift her head, feeling the scaly dryness of the hair that is dyed to be a match for mine. She shifts and whimpers, still semi-conscious, and I whisper, "There now, there." I manoeuvre the bag all the way around, slowly, gently. I carry on murmuring, "It's alright, everything's going to be fine."

I hold the end open a short while longer, allowing her to continue her unlaboured breathing, to drift more firmly down.

Then I make my move, working deftly, drawing the drawstring securely to a close, tying a single knot and tightening it. Her hands flutter, but they lack direction and resolve.

I step away and I watch.

She continues breathing, the rise and fall of her chest easy, as she uses up the air in the bag, replacing the oxygen with carbon-dioxide, her body supplying its own poison. I watch as her breathing starts to stutter and her hands float upwards.

I watch, every muscle tense. Her fingers are tugging at the string, her bitten nails clawing at the toughened plastic. Her body half rises, struggling to sit up, reaching towards me in supplication and I can see her contorted features through the semi-opaque film, the grotesquely gaping mouth, the wide eyes. I hear the animal keening in her throat.

My own breath catches too and I press my hands determinedly against my thighs, stopping myself from acting, from pinning her arms down, or grabbing a pillow, or from undoing the knot, focussing so hard on the effort of staying put that I hardly know what it is I want.

Images canter through my mind.

I think of how it began, a trifling encounter with a stranger, of helping her up from where she'd slipped and fallen in the snow and inviting her into my flat to warm up with a cup of tea. Back when I thought myself a decent person.

I think of flowers, cards and gifts, of poems with their adolescent avowals of undying love, fripperies that I tried to laugh away, though they unnerved me. Of phonecalls in the middle of the night and a hundred times a day and being ambushed outside my office. Of photos left on my windscreen depicting severely beaten up women. Of break-ins and small personal items going missing. Of death threats sent to Mike, which the police could never trace. Of crying at my niece's christening because I suddenly understood that I could never have a child, it would be far too great a risk. Of Mike on the hospital ward, the hollows of his cheeks, the bruising of his jaw, more shaken than hurt by the hit and run. And later, him saying he was sorry, but he couldn't do this anymore, it wasn't so much the threats, but that I had changed and what was good between us had got lost. Of restraining orders and their persistent violation, of arrests and trivial sentencing that had no impact.

Of the cycle of running, waiting and being found.

I watch and wait while time stutters and stalls, stretching itself out so minutes pass like hours, pass like

81

days. Her hands weaken to moth-wings batting against glass.

I have one last chance to reconsider.

To wonder if finally she *gets it*. Whether amidst the befuddlement of drugs and panic, she recognises the truth and knows how much I hate her.

Or whether, even now, she considers this as one last trial, the ultimate opportunity for her to prove how worthy she is of my love, how immutable her adoration, no matter what cruel tests I set.

I stand unmoving, cast in stone, and listen to her rasping breaths, my final chance passing beyond reach. I watch the slow, painful process of death, stealing away this pathetic creature who so desperately believed that love would make her whole.

She is still. Inside me is a void. I feel no pity, not for her, not even for myself.

I breathe in deeply, then proceed. I place the scrubbed vial of pills in her palm and press her fingers lightly closed then let the bottle fall. My cleaning cloth runs over the surfaces I have touched. I find her mobile by the bed. I gather up the tumbler and plate I used, and my Tupperware box. I unpin every last scrap of her warped shrine. I place everything in another of those garden sacks.

I close the door behind me as I leave, crossing fingers that it might be several days before the lock is forced.

I think ahead to how I will dump the sack in the canal, pick up my belongings from the hall, push the keys back through the letterbox and head for the railway station.

All sorts of things could give me away. Myriad clues might alert the police to the suspicious nature of her death. Her medical and criminal records will show the link to me. Who knows what traces of DNA I may have left behind, what images CCTV might have captured. As for my vanishing act, well *she* has always managed to find me.

Or perhaps it is my turn for luck, the universe re-establishing a karmic balance. The police might be disinterested, not bothering to probe beyond the apparent suicide.

I have no way of knowing, and doubt will continue over days, weeks, even years. But I have got used to waiting and this time, at least, the pattern is not fixed; I do not know how it will begin.

This time, the future lies open.

About the author:
Sarah Evans has had dozens of stories published in magazines, competition anthologies and online, including by: the Bridport Prize, Unthank Books, Bridge House Publishing and *Writers' Forum*. Recently her story *Acclimatising* won the inaugural Winston Fletcher prize. She has also had work performed in Faversham, Hong Kong and New York.

Hush

Melanie Whipman

She's crying. They do it every time. Ten to one. I'll be smiling, telling them everything's just fine. No need to worry. But they cry anyway. When I haven't even touched them. This one is just the same. "Hush, hush," I say.

Mum used to cry when Dad left. Night after night, with the moonlight barring her duvet and her face hot and snotty in my neck. In the daytime she'd push me away, would get on her knees and scrub the floor, her hands ungloved, raw with heat and bleach. Every once in a while she'd stop, rest her bottom on her heels and pull a hankie from her pocket; a monogrammed piece of cotton, ironed as flat and smooth as a cross-word square.

She used to boil them up in our pasta pan, then dry them on the radiator like rows of little flags. Afterwards she'd stack them up on the board. I remember the hot hissing of the iron under her two handed hold. "Run and get me a penguin, Carly boy," she'd say. She had a sweet tooth. I'd feed her while she ironed. Portions of penguin popping in. "Pick, pick, pick-up a-penguin, pop-it-in," she'd sing. I'd post them in, above those blue-white pristine squares. No crumbs. I was very careful.

She'd smile. "Cruel to be kind, Carly boy?" She'd lift the iron and make it hiss.

When Dad left she'd hold them to her face and grind them up in snotty, sodden balls. She'd blub out words that women shouldn't say. She'd scream out names. "Slut! Bitch! Slag!"

I never say it to my girls. I wipe away their tears with a hankie from the haberdashery section at John Lewis. There are drawers full of them – cotton, silk, plain, embroidered, layered up in squares and triangles – enough for the world's tears.

The girls' faces are always smudged. I smooth away their masks. Make them clean again.

I was Mum's rock when Dad left. Me at her side, sharing cuddles and Penguins. No crumbs. "Hush, hush." She'd kiss the iron-shaped scar on my cheek and hold me close.

"You can read it if you want to." She'd hold up Dad's letter.

Carl Redman, on the envelope, in neat capitals, his writing alien, small and unimportant. I used to watch Mum's face. "D'you love him?" she'd say.

"No, no."

"Maybe he wants you to visit him," she'd smile, "him and that slut."

I never made a mistake, "No thanks," I said, her loyal soldier.

We'd burn them. Swan matches, yellow and red, the scraping smell of sulphur and the paper flaring up. "Careful of your hands, love!" she'd giggle.

We'd watch the unseen words shrink to a pile of grey flakes in the guest ash-tray.

"Ashes to ashes, dust to dust, hush, hush," she said.

They slowed to a trickle, then sporadic drops, then one day stopped. When there were no more white envelopes on the Monday morning mat she held me close, "Typical," she said, "no stamina."

"My name's Jo," this one says, through lips all fat and shiny with crying. Like squashy, slimy, slugs. "What's yours?" she says.

85

I want to laugh. Hands wired, trussed up like a fucking Tesco chicken, and she's trying psychobabble. But it's the name that really does it. Joe! If only she knew.

Joe Mendocks ran the local garage. I'd fill up Mum's car, and out he'd come, "Hi Laura!" Wiping his greasy, groping mitts on his overalls. Grease stains like crushed insects all over.

"Fancy an ice?" he asked

Like he was in a fucking American movie.

So there was Joe washing the windscreen, me filling up, both watching Mum lick her Magnum, lips ringed in chocolate, like some obscene shade of lipstick.

"Thanks Joe," she said, all shimmies and smiles.

I drove off, silken smooth, careful as a cat.

"Do you like him, Mum?" I asked

"Who darling?"

The girl's still snivelling, swallowing and chewing her cheek, trying to speak. I've seen it all before.

"I've got a little boy."

I flap the handkerchief at her, "Shh, hush, hush."

I can smell urine, sharp and stagnant above her flowery perfume.

She soldiers on. "He's five, just five."

I was five when Dad left. She had to be strict, a single mum. Cruel to be kind.

"D'you have a family?" Her face is all puffy, eyes red, like that dinner lady from Denby. I hold up the can of petrol, wave it under her nose. "Not any more," shaking the can, sloshing it round. "Whoosh!"

Ten years it was just the two of us. Then along comes Joe. Mum started wearing heels. Click-clacking across the parquet. Then he moved in. I like remembering the Vesta flares and the speed of the greedy flames, gobbling up the house. And Mum's iron melted on the blackened tiles. I never could get that clean.

The girl starts yabbering, and I've had enough. I drag the chair towards the cellar door. Her heels scrabble at the floor, pecking for a purchase in the parquet, like the others.

I've got a box of heels somewhere, cowboy boots, stilettos...

"He's only five, my little boy."

This one's wearing flat boots and a flowery skirt in a corded material and the kind of thick woollen tights that school kids wear. They're normally screaming by now, but this one keeps talking.

"He'll be waiting for me to tuck him in."

At this stage I've heard it all, been offered everything – money, sex, religion.

"He's called Carl," she sobs, "I read to him."

I'm at the cellar door and I've got the petrol and the Swans and the hankie in my hand.

Carl.

"The one about the mocking bird."

And she starts singing, her voice hoarse, "Hush little baby, don't say a word, Papa's gonna buy you a mocking bird..."

She's crying and singing. The words hiccoughing out. I hold the hankie up, rattle the matches, slosh the can.

But she carries on singing.

I've gotta say, singing's a first.

Mum used to say, "We have to adapt." Maybe a bit of flexibility's needed here. And I'm not superstitious, but what with Joe, and Carl, maybe it's a sign. I let the chair drop and stuff the hankie in my pocket. My rubber soles squeak as I walk away. It's about time I moved on. Plenty of other towns. I wonder, just for a second, about 'her

Carl' and what it would be like to be him, to feel the weight of her tipping your mattress, her cool hand on your forehead and her low, steady voice hushing you to sleep.

About the author:
Melanie Whipman grew up in Brighton, and has lived in Germany, France and Israel. She has now settled in a Surrey village with her husband, teenage twins, dog, cats and chickens. She has an MA in Creative Writing and her short stories have been published in various magazines and anthologies and broadcast on Radio 4. She is a PhD student and an associate lecturer at the University of Chichester. Her short story collection will be published next year by Ink Tears.

I'm Still Me, Puss

Madeleine McDonald

"Not now, puss," she told him as he greeted her, tail erect. "You're a nice puss, but if I sit down and stroke you, I'll never get up again. I need my bed."

As she walked into the kitchen, the first thing she saw was a vase of fresh tulips on the table, a mixture of yellow and red blooms, with a note trapped underneath. "Shepherd's pie in fridge. Have taken ironing home. Love you lots, Mum."

Love you lots too, Mum. Tears stood in her eyes but the cat snaked round her legs, demanding attention. Even though Mum had been, she checked his food and water bowls. That much at least she owed him. She could not bear to give him away, not yet. His presence filled the flat, and the family downstairs had promised to give him a home.

"We adopted you from the rescue centre instead of having a baby," she informed the cat. "Just as well, the way things turned out."

Dominic had abandoned them both for a new life in Australia. *You can't ask me not to take the job. It's my big chance.* Holly had emailed him, but had received no answer. So much for Dominic deserving to know. She imagined him as embarrassed by the news of her condition as the teenage son from downstairs, who gulped whenever he saw her, and slunk by with a muttered greeting.

She fumbled with the buttons of her coat. They felt heavy and awkward, catching in the thick fabric. She leaned on the worktop and took a breather before she tugged the strap of her handbag over her head. The move dislodged the knitted hat, and she caught a glimpse of herself in the mirror. Her eyes were drawn to the bald crown that eclipsed all other features.

She leaned forward, examining her reflection. "I'm still here. I'm still me." She said it aloud, for emphasis. "This is still my flesh, these are still my bones." She breathed on the surface of the mirror, drew a heart shape in the little patch of mist, and watched it fade. "My heart is still in service. Not that I can feel it, but I'm still here, so it must be working." She traced the lines where once her eyebrows had grown. Below them, eyes stared back. Same eyes, different frame.

The baldness did not upset her. In the first stages of chemotherapy, Holly had attempted to trim and set what was left of her hair, buying a special baby brush for the purpose. Then one day she turned up with a bottle of wine and an electric razor. "We'd better do this while we're both sober," she joked, before attacking the remaining clumps.

It had been a good day when she had shed the last of her hair. It was surprising how liberated she felt once the deed was done. *Move over Sinead O'Connor, I'm in control here.* Afterwards, one of Mum's friends had knitted her a selection of woolly hats to match her favourite outfits.

It was the invisible changes that devastated her, the ones deep inside, and those changes were so frightening she could not talk to anyone. "I'm still me. I can't be an old woman, not yet." She told the cat what she could not bear to tell her friends. "I'm twenty-eight and inside I feel eighty-two."

To avoid her reflection, to avoid the haggard eyes that told her she was eighty-two, she backed away and sat down. The cat approached and placed its front paws on her thigh, back paws poised to jump. "Come on then." She lacked the energy to push him away. She lacked the energy to get up and go to bed. Weakness invaded muscle, sinew and bone, leaching them of vigour and purpose. Lassitude paralysed her desires.

Once on her lap, the cat thrust his head into her elbow. She felt rather than heard his purr, along with the welcome warmth he generated. From her thighs and belly, the vibrations rippled into the furthest reaches of her battered body, subduing the mangled heartbeat, confronting the defeated citadels of bone, scoffing at their feeble defences.

Insidious at first, the vibrations became insistent. The more her body surrendered to them, the further inwards they rippled. Their message was one of insolent health. "Caress me," they commanded. "Feel my warm breath. Trace the outline of my sprawled body. Stroke my soft fur. But mind you do so with gentle fingers, for I do you a favour lying here at my ease."

The cat had no awareness of her illness, nor did he take any interest in her looks. "You don't care, do you?" she asked, scratching the curve of his back. "You know I'm still me and you know I'm the one who feeds you." She relaxed into his hypnotic purr and absorbed his egotism with gratitude, knowing he purred only because he was fed and pampered. "You won't miss me, not you." Sometimes the love and concern shown by friends and family overwhelmed her. *So much love that I can never repay.*

After giving the matter much thought, she had slipped a handwritten note inside her will, asking Mum to make sure that Jo got her old-fashioned garnet ring, and Holly the framed watercolour of Whitby. Whitby had been one of their favourite weekend destinations: fish and chips on the pier, followed by an afternoon exploring the craft shops.

How long would her keepsakes be valued? Mum would weep forever. But would Jo think of her every time she wore the ring, any more than she herself thought of the long dead great-grandmother who had once owned it? Would Holly mislay the picture of Whitby in some future house move?

91

Holly and Jo would have their own families one day. She tried to imagine them at her mother's age, grown plump and cuddly. It was impossible. She saw them only as they were now, generous, upbeat and assertive. Tears took her by surprise. She remembered the day they had let themselves into her flat, advanced on the haggard creature in the mirror, and seized that poor creature by the elbows. Supporting her one on each side, they marched her out into the sunlight – as if willpower alone could effect a cure.

Despite their best efforts, her flat would soon be empty. Jo and Holly would probably clear it out to save Mum the heartache. For how many months would they drink to her memory, even as some tiny part of their mind registered the arrival in the pub of an attractive man? Multi-tasking, the three of them used to call it, when they caught one another doing it.

Life goes on. It seemed fitting to envisage Jo and Holly turning their energies to new challenges. It seemed fitting to imagine the cat settling comfortably into a new home. She tried to imagine Dominic married, bringing up a family in faraway Australia, perhaps taking his kids surfing, but the only image that came to mind was his edgy fidgeting the day they said goodbye at the airport.

"Sometimes it's good to be selfish like you, puss," she told him. "And sometimes not. It's a question of balance."

The answer was a deep purr. Its lullaby comforted her as life ebbed from her battered frame.

About the author:
Madeleine McDonald lives on the Yorkshire coast, where the wind whistles up through the floorboards. She finds inspiration walking on the beach.

That's The Spirit

The Viking

The ghost of Eddie Sartori, late of Chicago's criminal underworld, floated around a squalid apartment illuminated by fluorescent advertisements from the street below. On a coffee table lay a release order from the Illinois State Penitentiary granting liberty to Leonard Aaron Levy who lay asleep on a sweat soaked mattress. It was the hottest summer for fifteen years; even the birds were tanned.

Closely examining Lenny's pallor, the ghost came to a decision. "He'll do, his prison tan says it all; fresh out of poky and down on his luck; the perfect fall guy." The ghost de-materialised before dawn ushered in another glittering day in the Windy City.

The spook returned the following night just as Lenny was preparing for bed. He snatched a Glock hand-gun from beneath his pillow, screaming, "Back off or I'll ventilate you; you schmuck."

"At least the sap ain't yellow," observed the visitor disregarding the firearm. It coasted toward the ex-con attempting to insert its forefingers into his ears. Lenny shrieked and emptied his gat into the ghost's head.

Unperturbed, it drifted over to write an ectoplasm message on a grimy wall mirror with a finger. It read, "I'm a ghost and can only communicate with you by plugging my fingers into your listeners. It's to do with the living and the dead having different atomic oscillation levels; or *sumpun* like that."

Inquisitively Lenny limped to the mirror laboriously tracing each glowing word with a finger. He turned to the hovering wraith and said slowly, "Okay, Smokey Joe, but warm up your fingers *foist* with that ectoplasm stuff you guys are made of."

The ghost wrote in reply, "They don't do warm fingers where I come from, pal, cos we ain't flesh an' blood nomore, and anyhow, ectoplasm's no warmer than a hooker's price list."

"Okay, plug-in, but tell me who you are and what you want or I'll blow you away with my electric fan," sniggered Lenny becoming more confident.

"Electric fan, huh?" said Sartori after plugging in to Lennie's ears, "Listen wise guy, you ain't so smart or you wouldn't have tried to whack a ghost with a hand-gun. But grinding you down ain't why I'm here. My name's Sartori, Eddie Sartori. Now *lemme* ask you *sumpun*; what's with the limp?"

"Aw I got mixed up in a streetcar accident as a kid, and my right leg ended up shorter than the other; what's it to you anyhow?"

"I wanna know if you can drive an automobile."

"Sure can, I own a Packard convertible," Lenny announced with pride, "I've had the accelerator pedal built up to meet my bum leg."

"Good thinking, you'll make the White House one day. Now I'll tell you about myself, I got whacked in a shootout with the Paddy Feeney mob in 1928."

Awash with hero worship Lenny squeaked, "You mean you're t*he,* Eddie Sartori? Gee whiz, you're a legend in this borough."

Sartori grinned, "But I gave Feeney as good as I got, see; I blew him to confetti *wid* my Thompson."

Lenny's eyes glowed. "Holy cow, I ain't never fired a machine gun in my life; some guys have all the luck."

Encouraged by the adulation Sartori crowed, "And I

got voted hoodlum of the year in the *Racketeer* magazine and my name was always in the *Detroit Bugle*. But that's all in the past. Listen, this'll slay you. On my way up to the Pearly Gates to be judged, I met a swell ole guy sitting on a cloud wearing a long white beard and a halo around his noodle. I figured he was the welcoming committee cos he had on a clean *nightshoit.* So that's what I call him, *Nightshoit,* cute ain't it?" He gives me a look with the coolest grey eyes you ever saw and says, "You've got to repent for your life of crime and axe for *moicy,* Edward before you get da handshake. Once you've shown you're on the level you'll be allocated a harp and wings on condition you donate your ill-gotten gains to charity."

"See, Levy, during prohibition I hijacked liquor convoys for my speakeasies and cat houses, but getting a shout from a cop on my pay-role warning the Feds were planning a raid, I scrammed and buried my boodle in a graveyard. But the joke's on me see, cos this bone orchard's now under a bank called, The Wisconsin Bank of Foreign Trading. That's W.B.F.T to you and I need a buddy with an automobile to help me transfer the dough to a charity; and that's where you come in."

"Whoa, whoa, fog face, not so fast; what do I get out of this?"

"That's already been taken care of, kiddo," said the crook, "*Nightshoit* says if you keep your nose clean he'll allocate you a swell singing voice when you snuff it so you can trill with his angels at your own funeral service; how's that for a novelty? Better than stoking the bad boy's furnace for less than a dime an hour; ain't it?"

"Gee, that's sure *sumpun*," admitted Lenny. "Well I ain't drilled no-one, and I only knocked over liquor stores when times *wuz* rough; maybe I can get a better deal by going straight. I might even meet a swell broad and rear a bunch of rug-rats; okay, hot shot, count me in."

"Suckered," rejoiced his exploiter. To Lenny he grated, "Okay partner, park your heap near the W.B.F.T before dawn tomorrow, and bring a broom and shovel cos you're going into the street cleaning business."

An hour before sun-up, Lenny parked his Packard carefully in a side street next to the W.B.F.T, and guided by Sartori, he took his broom and shovel down a steep spiral stairway leading to a plaza and the subterranean strong-room of the W.B.F.T beneath which lay the graveyard containing Sartori's loot.

"Slow down, ya bobbin' slob, no city street cleaner ever moves that fast," said Sartori trailing from Lenny's ears "Take it easy; hum an Al Jolson number or *sumpun*."

"Hum it yourself, it ain't you that'll get busted if the bulls show," Lenny replied.

Sartori thrust his nose into Lenny's face and sneered, "Use your noodle, Levy, be inventive, come up *wid* a convincing story like you're from the City Cleansing Department sweeping up twigs for the city's, 'Save the Beavers' campaign on the Illinois river,' and after the cops have scrammed I'll melt into the graveyard and throw the bags up to you. Just look dumb like normal and stick to your story."

"You're *axin*' for a smack in the teeth," said Lenny throwing his tools down with a clatter.

The apparition groaned, "Knock it off, bone-dome, be positive; you'll be singing like Caruso one day without it costing you a cent. Now listen, there's fifty grand in five bags, so bring your heap down on the plaza service road and keep your eyes peeled; it'll be a push-over."

"Thanks a million, Sartori, this show gets better by the minute," Lenny said. "Supposing the bulls see through the

96

beaver story; they ain't all knuckleheads y'know."

"Then come up with *sumpun* like you won the Mexican lottery and wanna make a donation to the police fund when the W.B.F.T opens. But please, Lenny baby, don't pull your rod on the nice men in blue or they'll shoot you deader than Coolidge's donkey."

A vein throbbed on Lenny's forehead, "But what if they ain't *hoid* of the Mexican lottery? They'll throw me in the poky while you float away in the breeze you dirty double crosser."

"Merciful heavens, Leonard, how distrustful of you," said Sartori. "Listen, jackass, if that happens I'll never get the dough to get me out of the jam I'm in; so I'll lose out too." Shaking his head in despair, he faded into the bank's foundations as his patsy Lenny limped off to pick up his auto...

The first mouldering bag shot through the wall slamming into Lenny's midriff. He lugged it into the trunk of his car, dealing with the rest in quick succession.

Sartori emerged shaking with laughter as he plugged into Lenny's ears. "Hey, kid, I just ran into one of Gilbert the Limey's boys propping up the bank's foundations. Feeny's mob gave him a concrete overcoat for dealing off the top at a poker game and he wants *Nightshoit* to cut him a deal cos he's been going straight ever since..."

Ten minutes earlier, a police cruiser had stopped outside the bank; the crew loosening their collars in the stifling heat. The driver croaked, "Say what won the Nantucket Derby yesterday Danny?"

"Southern Belle, won by five lengths," his buddy grinned, studying a figure down on the dimly lit plaza hefting money bags into the trunk of a convertible. He gulped, "Hey, Max, get a load of that guy down on the plaza, someone's pitching money-bags to him, through the wall of the W.B.F.T."

Max revolved his head like an owl to get a better look. "Holy Moses," he yelped, "and there goes *anudder* one; what is this guy; a magician?" The cops pounded to the top of the stairway freeing their side-arms...

Lenny loaded the last of the money-bags into the Packard, and disregarding the cops' warnings, put his foot to the floor leaving tyre burns on the road while Sartori re-connected to his ears. He screamed, "Make for the Racine road, Levy, you'll find a place called the Waifs and Strays Children's Care-Home a mile up on the right. Hand over the dough and let's beat it."

Fumbling his gears as he took a dog-leg bend too fast, Lenny lost control rolling the auto down an embankment close to the children's home.

In hot pursuit the police cruiser screeched to a halt with Max and Danny pulling Lenny clear of the wreckage; but he was bleeding profusely from the mouth.

"It's all over for me, guys," he choked, "I'm busted up good inside. The dough in the trunk's for the Waifs and Strays Children's home; I tried to go straight but it ain't *woiked* out that way." He coughed blood and peacefully died.

In the after-life Lenny was queuing outside the 'New Arrivals Settling in Accommodation, when Sartori floated by looking meaner than usual.

"Hey, Eddie," Lenny shouted, "how soon will I get that great singing voice you promised me?"

"Get lost, ya palooka, that was all hot air; just sumpun to reel ya in."

Lenny bridled, and breaking from the queue, rushed at

Sartori with clenched fists. A saintly figure materialised between the two pinning Lenny's arms to his sides. It said, "No violence is permitted here, Leonard. See, it's like this, I'm one of the big wheels around here, the one Sartori calls *Nightshoit*; and thinks I don't know about it." He grabbed Sartori by the lapels of his coat. "Listen you stumble-bum," he said, "we let you go earth-side to clear your name; but you let us down and got Lenny's curtains drawn."

Sartori whined, "But he died doin' *sumpun* good, boss."

"Yeah, and the dough went to charity; but I'm still kicking your butt for calling me *Nightshoit*; so you're taking over from Gilbert the Limey's hood under the W.B.F.T I'll throw in a loaded roulette wheel so you can cheat yourself at gambling; I ain't having no wiseacre saying *Nightshoit*'s a good guy gone bad." He turned to Lenny who stood round eyed and speechless. "And you, Lenny baby, now have a voice that'd melt a stack of silver dollars, and if you haul ass, you'll catch your burial service and get to sing with my angels like Sartori promised; but remember; I'm the guy who's making it happen." He shot a triumphant glance at the dishevelled hood, "Sometimes the *trute* is stranger than the friction; ain't that so, Sartori?"

About the author:
James Sainsbury, a former central heating quality control inspector, began writing in 1990 after completing a correspondence course, and had two articles and three short stories published. Upon retirement he noticed his two little fingers were curling into the palms and was told he had Dupuytren's Contracture; a disease brought over by the Vikings, hence his chosen pseudonym – The Viking – all five feet six inches of him; not your average berserker.

Mallinson's Angel

Ruby Cowling

There was nowhere like Mallinson's department store at Christmas. I've never known such dedication to *tradition*. Not only because the decorations were proper ones, with fairylight angels and the correct number of reindeer – none of those inflatable Santa Clauses, or those dreadful walking stick things – but because they would actually use the very same decorations year after year. I was with Mallinson's thirty-seven years, and the fairy lights they used in 2012 were the very same ones they used in 1975. Wonderful.

When I started at Mallinson's, it was just the one store, in Harrogate. Something special. I worked there before the nationwide expansion. Before the wedding list department. Before the television screens beaming down on everyone with their scrolling special offers. Before the slick orange army of Clarins girls, with their heels and their nails. We never really ran into each other on the shop floor, but we would always smile when we ended up having to get in the lift together. Those girls have a special customer-service smile that lasts a bit too long. They look as if there's an amusing tune playing in their heads that they know you can't hear.

I know how to do a proper smile for a customer. I was trained by Ralph Mallinson himself. "Make a smile, make a sale," he'd say, and in all those photos I had hanging in the stockroom, he had that smile of his. I don't know what they teach them these days. Oh, they can always work the modern computer systems, do it all in seconds, as if they were born to it, but not the rest of it. Not the Tradition of All-Round Respect, as he put it.

100

They were nice girls, don't misunderstand me, but it was as if there was a part of them that wasn't really *devoted*.

Take Siobhan, a former Clarins girl who somehow got transferred to Fragrances. Siobhan would ask for her break when she'd only been there forty-five minutes. She would loiter in the stockroom and fiddle with her mobile phone, letting a queue build. She would watch a customer sniff their wrist and say "Ooh, that's quite nice," and she'd say, "That one? Mmm. Reminds me of my Nan. She's in a home."

Ralph – Mr Mallinson – would have shuddered in his grave, God rest him, if he could have seen how she carried on.

She didn't *mean* any disrespect to him, of course. I told her all about him and his ethos when she first started, and at the end of my talk she said, "Whatever!" (That's young people's shorthand for "Whatever next!", which, I've worked out, is the equivalent of "I'm impressed!") And naturally, what with me being a more mature woman, there was a respect there. A regard. When I told her no, she had to wait for her break, she did wait. All she could do was slam the till drawer, and pop her chewing gum with this spitty little snap. There was no malice. When she went to the fridge and left that gum in my lunchbox, perching on my salad like a tiny grey turd, I knew it was just her way of teasing, saying *Look at us, working together, sharing the same space, we share a sense of humour, don't we?* Just a bit of fun.

There was one time I did have to admonish her. It was in the staff ladies' during *my* break, when I suddenly saw her head pop up over the top of the cubicle wall, and I was there with my – well, in a delicate position, with regards to hosiery and underthings – and I said, "Siobhan, stop it now, that's not funny." I think she got the message, because she climbed down more or less straightaway, once she'd finished fiddling with that phone thing she never put down.

But she never meant any real harm.

Christmas Eve last year we were busier than you can imagine. Our last half-day, then the traditional Mallinson's shutdown until the third of January, so I had to make sure we stayed professional and focused; no time for falling out, no room for bearing a grudge. "Make a smile, make a sale." Fragrances was like a station at rush hour – only with a base of musk, and floral top notes. Customers were crowding round as if they were starving and we were handing out food parcels. On that day, business needs required that I ask Siobhan to work through her morning break.

Then I started to notice customers pointing up at the television screens. I knew we were showing the two-for-one on Givenchy, but I couldn't understand why they kept looking at the screens, then nudging each other and looking again. So I stepped out from the Davidoff counter and had a look myself.

They all had the same picture, a still photo. From above, an old lady twisting to look up, with her eyes and her mouth open wide, bending forward to grab her underclothes from round her sagging white knees.

When I looked back, everyone was looking at me.

Just a bit of fun. Just youthful high jinks.

So I asked Siobhan to set the screens *back* to our Givenchy offer, and if she wouldn't mind, to delete that photograph altogether, thank you kindly.

And we worked until 12.30, and we closed up and cleared everything away into the stockroom, and said

102

goodbye to the Clarins girls as they left one by one. Then I put a forgiving hand on Siobhan's shoulder and thanked her for the day's work, and wondered whether she wouldn't like to choose something from the sample size bottles we keep up on the top shelf? And her narrow eyes lit up and she was on that ladder and up it, quick as you like. I had a bottle of Britney Spears *Curious* in my hand, and I'm still not sure how it got there; in fact I was so surprised to see it that I dropped it. It smashed of course, and poor Siobhan jumped, and that ladder almost went over but I stopped it! I steadied it with my hand. We shared a little look then, me and Siobhan, sort of a *phew* between ourselves, and a real smile, not a customer-service smile.

I could feel Mr Mallinson watching us from his photos. His girls, at Christmas, and the Tradition of All-Round Respect.

I needed to clean up all the bits of glass, of course, and it was gloomy in there. And poor Siobhan couldn't really see either. So I stepped out and pulled a couple of strings of those traditional fairy lights down from around the door. I picked up an illuminated Virgin Mary, the one who'd melted slightly around where the cable went in, and thought if I gave her wires a little tug she'd probably stretch far enough in so she could light things up, along with those fairy lights, which felt ever so hot. And do you know? When I stood the sizzling Virgin Mary in that puddle of Britney Spears *Curious,* at the bottom of Siobhan's ladder, she did light us up; in fact, she and the hot string of lights started sparking quite wonderfully.

Then I wished Siobhan a very happy Noel, and I pulled the stockroom door closed and locked it, and I went home for Christmas.

103

About the author:

Ruby Cowling grew up in West Yorkshire and lives in London.
Her publication credits include *The Letters Page*, *Unthology 4*,
The View From Here, and, in audio format, *4'33"* and *Bound
Off*. She won the 2014 White Review Prize and the 2013
Prolitzer Prize from Prole magazine, and was Highly
Commended in the 2012 Bridport Prize.
http://rubyorruth.wordpress.com

Marilyn's Alter Ego

Glynis Scrivens

It was typical of Jonathan to have a thing about Marilyn Monroe, Lisa thought.

There he was, sitting opposite her at the kitchen table, sipping his morning coffee, raising his mug in a silent salute to his idol, who smiled at him from the calendar, her skirt billowing around her shoulders.

He should know better at his age. Seventy, for goodness sake. Old enough to have grown out of this.

Old enough to know that women and gravity weren't the best of bedmates over time, as she bore testimony. Was that Marilyn's big attraction? He never had to watch her beauty decline, the wonderful blonde hair become thin and lose its bounce, the famous legs get cellulite. She'd always be young and gorgeous. Timeless.

"It's her birthday tomorrow," he confided.

"And it's mine next week. You'd do well to remember that."

Last year he'd actually forgotten. Not Marilyn's special day, of course, but Lisa's. The one who'd put up with his moods and his sometimes tenuous grasp of reality all these years.

For what, she sometimes wondered? Security? A roof over her head? Surely it came at a cheaper price?

No, she loved him. Silly Jonathan, with his calendars and his hangups. He'd walked into her life one day at the supermarket where she worked, and that was it. Her life changed the moment he approached her checkout.

There was something gentle and appealing about him. He seemed both strong and vulnerable, which intrigued her. She still remembered the contents of his shopping trolley. A double-layered chocolate cake, candles and a magazine. She'd noticed the smiling cover shot of Marilyn. He wasn't the first man to buy this issue.

"Somebody's birthday?" she'd said, scanning the barcode on the packet of candles. Noticing that he wasn't wearing a wedding ring.

"Marilyn's."

She'd liked the sound of his voice.

They'd started talking, and he'd invited her to coffee during her break. A few months later he'd won her heart.

Love was blind.

And possibly silly as well.

Was it Marilyn taking him to hospital today? Sitting with him while he waited for the results of his tests? Going to the cafeteria to bring them both a cup of tea and a cheese sandwich, if the wait was too long? Did Marilyn care that he was a diabetic? That he might have a tumour?

Where are my thanks? Lisa thought. I've spent my life watching my husband drool over a beautiful blonde. A cliché of male desire.

"You'll have to hurry," she said. "The appointment is in half an hour and there might be heavy traffic."

Jonathan showed no sign of having heard her. He was gazing at Marilyn, the mug of coffee still at his lips, a faraway expression in his eyes.

Was it fear, she wondered? He'd had a good innings, of course, the biblical three score and ten years. But naturally he wanted more.

And so did she. A few tears welled into her eyes as she wondered how she'd cope if the tests came back positive. She averted her face from him, and became absorbed in washing the breakfast dishes.

"It'll be another false alarm," he said, at last. "These

young blokes and their tests. Enough to make anyone tear their hair out."

She didn't contradict him. Last time it hadn't been a false alarm. Just a lucky reprieve. They'd caught the tumour in time, before it had time to propagate and do its worst in his delicate system.

Jonathan owed his life to the "young bloke" and his tests.

But he'd be the last to ever admit that.

She drove them to the hospital although it was only three blocks from their bungalow. It'd been raining heavily all night, and she didn't want him to slip again. Last time he'd been a bit wobbly after the tests, and had tripped over his shoelaces, sprawling across the pavement, grazing his wrists and elbows badly. He'd looked like a child who'd fallen off a bicycle. He'd always retained his boyishness, part of him refusing to grow up. It was an endearing quality, but sometimes it strained her patience.

She held his arm, as they walked up the slope to the main hospital entrance. How she hated the signs to the oncology section. It was like a waking nightmare to trace and retrace her steps with him every four months. Waiting to hear if their worst fears had come true.

Shaken and clumsy. It was so disempowering.

But the relief when the tests came back negative was breathtaking.

"It's very dreary here," Jonathan said, looking around the waiting room. The walls were light grey, and the carpet a darker shade of grey.

"Surely they could find a more cheerful colour?" Lisa said.

This morning, in the waiting room, there was a young woman holding a baby. Lisa's heart stopped in her mouth. It was unthinkable that either of these could be at risk. She sighed audibly when an older woman joined them, and the young woman squeezed her hand encouragingly. The woman looked across at Lisa, with understanding in her eyes. Neither of them said anything.

They'd only been sitting there ten minutes when Dr Jacobs came to the doorway and called Jonathan.

Another doctor called the older woman.

Lisa caught the eye of the young mother, and smiled.

"My mother's taken a photo of Clint Eastwood in with her for good luck," the young woman said. "I told her it was ridiculous, but she didn't care."

It seemed like a good opportunity to talk about the Marilyn Monroe calendars.

"At least Clint Eastwood is growing old like the rest of us," Lisa said. "My Jonathan seems to be in denial about age."

"Is that a bad thing?" the young woman asked. "Maybe it's what keeps him going?"

Lisa nodded. "He's come close to giving up a few times," she admitted. "Something seems to keep him going."

"My mum's the same."

"If this was a movie, they'd meet each other and fall in love," Lisa said. "You and I wouldn't matter. Just the power of attraction of two like souls. That's what the cameras would celebrate."

"Who are we to argue?"

"He forgot my birthday last year," Lisa said. She surprised herself by admitting this to a total stranger. The words just tumbled out, needing to be said.

"Maybe he was too wrapped up in his own troubles?"

"He remembered Marilyn's."

They stopped talking as the older woman came out again. She looked overwhelmed. Lisa wondered what the news was for her. It was hard to tell.

Then she forgot all about her, as Jonathan emerged.

"I'll live to celebrate Marilyn's birthday next year," he crowed in triumph.

Waves of emotion swept through Lisa's body. She felt her hands trembling as she hugged him in relief.

"What about those symptoms?" she asked. "And the tests?"

He looked sheepish. "Too much chocolate," he said, sounding much younger than his seventy years.

"Chocolate?" she echoed.

He didn't meet her eyes.

Instead of driving home, she headed to the nearby shopping mall, and steered him towards the boutique. The one where she'd seen the turquoise dress with charcoal beads on the bodice. Jonathan wasn't the only one who found temptations difficult to resist.

She sat him down on a wooden chair, and asked the assistant if she could try on the dress.

She was led to a small cubicle with an unforgiving mirror. Her fingers still trembling, she felt the silken material. Soft and lustrous, and probably not intended for a woman of her age. But she yearned for its beauty, and today felt she'd earned the right to wear it if only for a few moments.

To her surprise it fitted perfectly. It seemed to glide over her arthritic hips and sit gracefully over her full bosom.

Jonathan drew out his wallet as soon as he saw her. She'd peeped out of the dressing room area, to catch his eye. Not that she had any intention of actually buying the dress, but today she'd simply needed to feel womanly.

He was at the counter paying for it, even as she started to protest.

109

"It's your birthday next week, so no arguments," he said.

"Where would I wear a dress like this?" she asked weakly. She didn't want to take it off, but really, something sensible would surely be a better idea?

He gave a wicked smile. "I'm taking you to the movies next week on your birthday," he said "We're going to see Gentlemen Prefer Blondes."

"Don't you get enough of Marilyn with your darned calendars?"

"There's no such thing as enough of Marilyn," he chuckled. Then he reached over and held her hand, his eyes never leaving her face. "And that goes for you too."

It was as close as he'd come to a compliment lately.

Clutching the boutique bag with its precious contents, she walked back to the car with him. The sky had clouded over again, and the first drops of rain were falling, but neither of them noticed.

About the author:
Glynis Scrivens writes short stories, and has been published in Australia, UK, Ireland, South Africa, US and Scandinavia. She writes for *Writers' Forum* (UK). She has had articles in *Pets, Steam Railway, Ireland's Own, The New Writer* and *Writing* magazine. Her work has appeared in seven anthologies. She lives in Brisbane with her family and a menagerie of hens, ducks, dogs, lorikeets, and a cat called Myrtle.

'Mer'-ry Christmas

Helen Shay

Out there, where you are – sitting round a table, pulling your crackers – all this must seem strange. Murky, perhaps? Indistinct? Too… wavy? But here, for us, it's so normal. Not "murky" but 'mer-ky', I suppose. At least, I used to think so – before I met the boy.

He was just one of your many random boys out there. Only for me, he was 'the boy'. Now it's good that water surrounds me, comforts me and makes it all indistinct and wavy. It submerges me back here, in my world of Mer, where things are not always so mer-ry at Christmas, when memory rises like a blade of pain to pierce the surface and turn the water red. Good job, underwater no-one can see the tears.

"All I want for Christmas is you!"

Well, why not? What's wrong with a bit of seasonal romance? Why shouldn't I try out what the mistletoe might have to offer? I was fourteen at last, and sick of swirling around with my sisters – sick of being told, 'No, you can't sing pop songs instead of arias! No you can't cut your hair short! No, you can't have a *Wonderbra*!' I mean, at fourteen it's different. That's when you're on the cusp. I could feel the power flow into me like the sea into a harbour. Fourteen is not an age for 'can't!'

And of course, Mark was so fit. I spotted him first running on along the Ayrshire coast that raw December morning, whilst I was surfing the waves during my morning swim. I didn't mean to splash him really. It was totally by accident, honest.

"Hey, didn't see you there," he said.

111

Then he looked at me long and deep, as if to make up for not seeing me before.

"Baby, don't worry 'bout a thing...," I sang.

(I've always liked Reggie, ever since the family wintered that time in the Caribbean and I picked up so much of it listening to the beach parties.) Mark just smiled.

"Cos every little thing, is gonna be alright," I sang to myself.

Of course, for the first few meetings I couldn't tell him. About 'Mer' I mean, the world I'm from. Or the tail. Well, especially the tail. That would be guaranteed to freak him out on the first date. But then, I didn't have to tell him. Like I said, at fourteen you're on the cusp and that's when you get the power. You get to decide who – and what – you are.

The sisters didn't like me seeing Mark. Jealous or what? They threatened to tell Mum and Dad.

"Meranda's going crazy. Running around town after everything with legs, and even wearing legs herself!"

Well, that flipping tail (and how it does flip) gets in the way, especially when you're out for a snog. So I told them to go ahead and tell if they liked. Why should I care?

"Let's leave it for now. Give her time to come to her senses. Realise that a boyfriend is not just for Christmas," Marina said.

Just because she's the eldest, she always likes to think she's oh so sensible and knows it all. But I thought I was the one who knew it all. When you're fourteen, you're on the cusp and you get to choose. Pure power.

It's like floating in a lagoon. Suddenly you know it's all *'gonna be alright'*. Your spots will clear, your teeth will straighten and, if you keep doing the aqua-aerobics, your tum will go flat. This time all those New Year resolutions would be fulfilled.

So you lie back, as the wind kisses your face and you glide into a dream. Your body lengthens. Scaly skin smooths into flesh, fins divide into legs. Then you emerge as the girl that you are, the girl that you want to be. And that summer, all I wanted to be was Mark's girl.

I have to admit that it did get a bit awkward at times: when he asked why we always had to meet and say goodbye on the cliff top; or when he took me to that seafood restaurant. Well, I'd been playing snap with that lobster only the day before, so I was hardly going to eat him (even if he did cheat). Still, in general, it went like a dream with Mark. Or is that what first love always is? Just a dream.

"You're it, Meri," Mark kept telling me. I liked the way he shortened my name to 'Meri', and he made me feel that I was 'it', or something – or someone – at last.

The sisters still moaned every time I got back late to the rock pool.

"You always make such a noise when you dive in, it wakes us up."

Like I say, jealous or what? Especially Marina, who has all the makings of an old mermaid. She can't even pull a merman, never mind a real boy.

But then came the night when I had to make another choice.

"We're going home after the festivities, Meri. My parents have to get back to the city, and my school starts back in a fortnight. We only come up to the cottage here at Christmas and holidays."

I stared back at Mark in silence. Was this the end

113

then? So much for being his 'it' girl. Instead I was being dumped. But then he held out a small gleaming, golden band. What was he expecting? I gazed at it. It seemed too big for a ring, but was the most delicate bangle I'd ever seen – far better than those the sisters had looted from that Armada wreck, and even shinier than that blue pendant thing we found on *The Titanic*. I thought it was a bracelet at first, but then Mark knelt down.

"Oh, he's going to propose!" I thought.

But then he slipped circlet round my ankle. It was a perfect fit.

"I wanted you to have something to remember me by," he said. "And to remind you that you're mine, even when we're apart."

Then he launched into all this stuff about me spending Christmas Day with his folks and like me going to stay with him at Easter later on and how his parents were fine about it.

"Great!" I said. "Only my family usually head south for the tropics in January, then travel around throughout the year."

Well, Mark put on one of those 'guy' looks. You know, the 'oh, so I'm not number one in your life' looks, that boys do – 'guilt trip' looks. Only I did feel the 'guilt' – and let's face it, it's only with legs that you can 'trip'.

I looked down at the anklet glittering on my foot. I knew then that Mark, without knowing it, had after all 'popped the question'. Feet or fin? It was the choice I had now to make.

I was very quiet when I got back to the sisters that night. I slipped into the pool and curled up silent as a shrimp. The next morning, we got up to comb our hair and practise our singing as usual, but I just couldn't get into it (even

114

though, like most mermaids, I'm normally very good at my scales). I had to face it, I would miss the sisters, even Marina. I tried the Reggie, but that didn't cheer me up either.

"No woman, no cry..."

But I did. And the one perk about being a mermaid is there's so much water around, no one sees the tears.

The sisters just got on with decking the cove with seaweed and making Christmas cockle pudding. Marina threw in some silver coral pieces, like she always did. I whopped with delight to find one of those in my dish when I was a kid, but who cares about stuff like that when you're a teenager? I must admit the main cave looked pretty cool though with all those shells hung up and a few bits of tinsel here and there. We each had a massive conch we'd leave out for Father Poseidon to deliver presents – though every year, it was always a new comb. Mer-elders are not that imaginative when it comes to their daughters. Still, there's something warm and lovely about the predictability of traditions. Carol singing was my favourite. We'd go from rock to rock belting out the old favourites to any odd crustacean or amphibian who might listen.

'*Oh starfish of wonder, starfish of night,
Starfish with royal beauty bright....*'

But at fourteen, haven't you outgrown the old ways?

It was Christmas Eve when I next walked to meet Mark on the cliff top. I could feel the magic in the night, and knew that I could wish for whatever I wanted. It was in the pale light of that new moon, that I tasted the most sweet and sorrowful kiss I shall ever know.

"I'm sorry, I can't," I murmured, pressing the gold band into his hand. 'I'm not ready to be yours – or anyone's.'

115

Except perhaps mine, I thought, as I trod back alone over the damp, rippled sand. The sea glistened ahead of me, sighing out its comforting breath of soft surf, as it drew me nearer to it. I was fourteen, on the cusp and still full of power. Tomorrow was Christmas Day, a day of family celebration and new life. My legs flexed, then welded into one surge of strength, as I dived into the waves – swimming as fast as my tail would carry me, towards all that lay ahead.

About the author:
Helen Shay has won several writing competitions and had some work published.

She has an MA in Creative Writing and teaches creative writing with York University CLL. She also writes poetry and has been a guest spoken-word performer at Glastonbury Poets Tent – with mud-stains to prove it. She loves fantasy, admiring Philip Pullman in particular, and is currently writing a young adult fantasy novel.

The Kite

Paula R.C. Readman

In the clear night sky, the moon hung high above, like a silent watcher. Casting its long shadows over no man's land as Harry stood, saturated by the heavy dew, peering over the trench walls, watching, knowing at last that he could do his bit for King and country.

For so long, he had hated the faceless enemies. Night after night with his rifle held high, he watched, while all around, the sounds of bombs and gunshots thundered in the darkness, only punctuated by the screams of dying men.

He saw only gloominess reflecting in the endless dips and hollows that pitted the once beautiful landscape, caused by the bombs that fell as they tried to win back the land lost to them on other such nights.

Sometimes, he was sure he could hear them laughing above the sound of carnage.

"Are they laughing at us, George?" He ground the words out through clenched teeth to his comrade-in-arms at his side, before lifting his rifle higher and steadying his aim. "Good men are dying because of the likes of them? I see no fun in that!"

Anger tore through Harry's heart. His conscience would be clear; he would never allow another man to suffer, unlike the enemy. No, not until he saw the whites of their eyes would he fire a single shot.

"I know," George said patting Harry's shoulder, "but don't let them get to you." Stifling a yawn, he squeezed past him, "I'm off to get some kip, if the buggers let me."

At the first light of dawn, through the misty haze that hung over the few feet of no man's land, Harry caught sight of their ghostly shadows moving amidst the foggy vapour. With aching muscles in his back, the tops of his arms and legs, he tightened his grip on his gun while steadying his aim. His chest and head knotted as he felt his face grow hot as his temper inflamed by their disregard to the raging turmoil around them. He watched as they lazily drew on their cigarettes, sending up clouds of smoke while their muffled voices carried across the land to torment him.

One night, on watch, Harry became aware that the man, who stood with his gun pointing at him, was the same man who had been there on previous nights. He wasn't sure how he knew, he just did.

Was it the way the enemy stood, so still, unwavering in his aim? Maybe, it was the way he held his rifle, with just as much determination as he did, for that he respected him. Harry shivered suddenly aware that some sort of familiarity had passed between them.

The days passed into weeks and the summer became autumn. The dried soil soon became a sea of mud under foot as rain mixed with the blood of the men. Bullets and bombs rained down on them along with the last of the falling leaves from what was left of the bullet-ridden trees that edged the trenches. The stench of death mingled in the air, along with the decay of the year as the trees stood like wounded guardian angels with their limbs torn away as they tried and failed to protect the lost souls in their care.

Harry stared at them briefly and shivered, touched by their sadness. They reminded him of the large ancient oak trees that edged the fields and meadows of a long, forgotten world lost to him now. Warmed by thoughts of home washing over him, he tried to forget the damp that ate its way through the soles of his boots, and clawed up his legs. He shivered again, this time touched by the coldness of the racing wind that whistled along the trenches in its bid to escape the surrounding madness.

"Here's something to break the monotony, Harry."

Startled out of his thoughts, he turned to find George holding out a letter to him. "Thanks, George," he said, lowering his gun.

"God only knows what will kill us first, the boredom, stench, rats, or mud. Sometimes, I doubt the enemy will get a look in. What do you think, Harry?" George said, squelching his way along the trench to the next man.

Wiping his hands on his jacket sleeve, he used his knife to slit open the letter. Guilt flooded him, with each word he read.

Dearest son,

I hope this letter finds you well. I'm sorry it's short, but I've been busy helping in fields. Dad has more than enough work to keep ten men going. It's been a good harvest this year, with a high yield. Though Tom is getting to be a big lad, he's not strong or tall enough to swing a scythe.

I'm hoping that I'll find the time to write you a good long letter soon.

Must go now, my dearest, Harry.

Watch out for a parcel, we sent one, but maybe you have already received it. Please don't say you don't have time to write, if it's only a post card, I will be satisfied. Are you in the trenches again?

Dad & Tom send their love. Keep safe & make haste to come home.

Mother X

Folding the letter carefully he slipped it into a waxed paper envelope with the others, and tucked it into his breast pocket, hoping to keep them safe and dry, before picking up his gun again.

Focusing on the enemy's line once again, he reasoned that his father needed him far more than his King did. Surely, the country needed him to plough the fields and harvest the crops to feed them during this time.

That last Sunday, a lifetime ago, the family had gone to church before they waved him off to join the army along, with many other young men from their village. He still could feel the sweetness of his mother's embrace as she kissed him goodbye. Tom just a kid, at eleven, he was too young to die for King and country and of little help to his parents too. Harry had been relieved that his mother would not lose both her sons to the war as she proudly stood waving him goodbye.

The hardest thing Harry had found was trying to snatch sleep at anytime during the day or night. When given notice to leave his post, he'd hurried dog-tired back to his bunk. Carved into the trench wall, the shelter of the bunk hadn't the power to block out the noise to allow his body to slip peacefully into the arms of Morpheus as the world screamed for him to stay and fight.

When his exhausted body and mind finally gave into sleep, he dreamt of home. He felt the warmth of a sweetly perfumed summer breeze across his bare back as he bent hoe in hand, helping his father.

Tom, thin arms and legs, ran like the wind he chased, across the field at the back of the house, with a homemade, paper kite, in tow. In the yard, he saw their mother standing tall and slender, her black hair swept up and pinned in place. At her hip, she held a basket from which she tossed grain to hungry clucking chickens that gathered round her feet.

Catching sight of the kite riding on the warm air currents above her head, she shielded her eyes, and looked up in time to see the kite dancing on the perfect, summer breeze.

Father resting a while, straightened too, before leaning on his hoe. A deep, caring chuckle broke the silence between them as they worked.

"I see the lad has made another one. My, my, that boy has determination, I'll give him that." He turned, and Harry felt his father's strength as he patted him on the back. "You, my lad, are strong both in mind and in character. I'm so proud of you both." With that, his father carried on with his toil as though nothing had happened. As the power of his father's love and pride flooded through him, Harry felt himself smiling, knowing his father was not one for fancy words.

A terrifying scream tore Harry from his father's side as the dream faded. Startled awake, he almost fell from his bunk. For a moment, he lay stunned by the agonising noise, his breath catching in his throat. His heart hammered in his chest as he tried to open his eyes, but something wet and sticky covered them.

At first, he thought, he was screaming. Terrified, he wiped at his eyes, realising that the stuff covering his face was the cause of his sudden blindness. Now that he could see, he looked down at his hands, to his horror, saw the blood, and checked himself.

It wasn't his.

A scream rang out again, piercing, pitiful and nearby.

Harry peered over the side of his bunk and found a boy lying in the mud.

"Tom?" he heard himself saying.

The boy's head turned slowly. Then with pleading baby blue eyes and a lost expression, he stared up at him.

Harry stood, trying to catch his breath.

The round, soft-faced boy-child, looked no more than seventeen; lay where he had fallen with half his body torn away. What was left of his torso sat propped up against the wooden bargeboard of the trench wall. Between the boy's legs, his guts spilled out snake-like in a pool of red and white matter across the duckboards mixing in with mud and dirt from where the bomb had blasted the trench wall away.

Transfixed by the fallen boy, Harry felt a sense of tranquillity even though all around the sounds of the big guns continued to rain chaos and hellfire down on them.

Harry stared fascinated at seeing no sign of pain or tears in the boy's eyes as he held up his hand to him. Dropping to his knees beside him, he took it and leaned forward to hear him plead, "Help me, Mister. I can't move my legs."

"I'm sorry Lad, there's nothing I can do, but pray to God for you."

The boy closed his eyes.

Relief washed over Harry, believing the boy must have slipped away to somewhere far more peaceful.

With a low groan, the boy opened his eyes again.

A sickening bile rose in Harry as he realised what he had to do. Then the boy suddenly spoke his thoughts aloud.

"Please kill me, Mister. I beg you. I can't stand the pain or noise anymore."

Harry closed his eyes in a silent prayer as he heard the boy cough.

Opening his eyes, Harry stared into the boy's eyes as thick, red blood oozed from between his pale lips. Without a second thought, Harry lifted his revolver to the boy's head.

A gentle smile flickered across the boy's thin bloodless lips, and Harry heard him say, "Oh, thank you, Mister. I can go home now."

The sound of Harry's revolver echoed around the trench, and seemed to block out the roar of the big guns too. Lowering his gun, Harry felt a tear roll down his cheek, and quickly wiped it.

Startled by a voice from behind him, he flopped back on his bunk, as a brother in arms pushed by him.

"Poor sod, isn't much else we could've done for the little bugger. Don't you go worrying yourself. It's what he wanted. None of us would be that lucky. Come on, George, give us a hand. We'll see if we can find a hole somewhere for him. You've done enough, Harry; you're a braver man than I'll ever be."

Harry stared at the gun in his hand, and tossed it away aware that he hadn't killed one of the faceless enemies, but a boy. Shot as though he'd been nothing more than a lame dog.

Putting the revolver back in its holster, Harry picked up his rifle, and took his place back at his post. As he looked across no man's land, he saw his enemy at his post on the far side, his gun focused on him. No longer did he watch with a keen eye, or hold his gun with a steady aim; he hadn't the stomach for it.

Laughter echoed along the trenches. Perplexed Harry looked around to see where it came from. Suddenly aware it came from his trench, he curled his lips in disgust, "Had everyone forgotten so quickly? Are we so numbed by death that we no longer care about one of our own?"

He lifted his gun, and stared across to no man's land.

Confusion filled the blood-scented air as Harry became aware that his enemy no longer stared at him, but stood staring up at the blue sky, with his hand shielding his eyes from the autumn sun. Harry lowered his rifle slightly, and followed his gaze until he saw what had caught his attention.

There fluttering over no man's land, high up in the clear, blue sky, hanging on the warm current was a white kite. Its brightly coloured tails seemed to dance in numerous twists and turns as the wind dipped and flowed.

Slowly, along the trenches on both sides the men of the frontline began to shield their eyes and look skywards, before nudging their comrade to look. Harry followed the string to earth and found no one held the kite. He checked the frontline again, reasoning aloud, "Surely someone held it."

Glancing at his enemy, he watched him gesture with a shrug of his shoulders that he too was puzzled. Harry found himself smiling, and returned the gesture.

In that moment, he wondered what else he shared with the enemy. After all, they were both men with parents and maybe siblings too.

Did he watch the kite in the same way as him? Had he spent time with his father, in a garden, in some distant time and place? Maybe he too had a kid brother, who played with a kite on a long hot day, when the world rested peacefully in some past life.

Harry put down his gun, and climbed over the top of the trench. Standing with his arms outstretched, he walked towards the enemy line.

"Come back you stupid bastard! You'll get yourself killed!" behind him his men called with anxious voices, but he kept on walking.

He passed by fallen, broken bodies of men from both sides. They stared up vacant-eyed at the white kite with its crucifix-style cross of thin canes as the mud did the only decent thing on the battlefield as it tried to swallowing them up.

Suddenly, the guns fell silent as Harry stood in the heart of no man's land staring up at the dancing kite. Then out of the opposing trench came the familiar stance as his faceless counterpart stood and walked towards him with his arms outstretched. In the middle of all the madness, two men embraced like old friends.

No words spoken. There wasn't any language left to express the sorrow, or anguish felt by both men. As his adversary took his hands in his and pulled him down onto his knees, Harry sensed what the unknown soldier wanted, and placed his hands together, closed his eyes, lifted his head towards heaven, and offered up a prayer to God for all the lost souls on the battlefield.

The man pull him Harry to his feet then after embracing him tightly for a few moments he held him at arm's length.

Harry found himself staring deep into the soldier's sky-blue eyes, and then a deep sense of peace wash over him. For a brief moment he was sure he saw the reflection of the dancing white kite with its fluttering multicoloured tail in his eyes, though he wasn't sure how.

With another quick embrace, the man turned, and walked away.

Just as Harry returned to his trench, he glanced back over his shoulder, and noticed that both the soldier and the kite were gone. Stunned for a moment, he became aware too that the big guns with their dragon-like mouths roared fire as the sounds of war filled the air with death once more.

"Wake up, Grandpa!" The excited child called, rushing into the quiet study from the garden.

"Hush, dear my child, you'll startle Grandpa," came the softly spoken voice of a woman.

"But, Mama, he mustn't be late for church."

Harry opened his eyes slowly to see his grandson watching him with bright, baby blue eyes and a soft baby-boy smile.

"Grandpa, I knew you were not asleep. You must be ready to go to work soon.

Harry laughed and sat up in his armchair before straightening his clerical collar.

"It's lovely to see you, Thomas, and your dear mother looking so smartly dressed and ready to come to church with me." Harry stood and embraced his daughter, before lifting his grandson to kiss his cheek.

The memories of the war to end all wars would never leave him. He knew it had marked him in so many ways, as it had done many others, but he'd been one of the lucky few who had survived.

Looking down into the bright eyes of his grandson, he hoped he would never have to take another man's life for either the right or wrong reasons.

"After church, grandpa can we fly my kite again?"

"Of course, we can, Thomas," Harry said ruffling his grandson's hair. "It looks to be the perfect day for it. Peaceful and just the right amount of summer breeze to make it dance."

About the author:

Paula R. C. Readman married to hard-working Russell, who allows her to follow her dream after English Heritage published her first short story in their anthology, *Whitby Abbey-Pure Inspiration*. Since 2010, she's had several other shorts published, and won two writing competitions, including having the best-selling crime writer; Mark Billingham select her story *Roofscapes* as the overall winner. She has a short gothic story published by Parthian Books.

Find out more about Paula on her Amazon Author page and blog: http://paulareadman1.wordpress.com

Save The Bum Tree

Athol Henry

Locals called the tree the Bum Tree, and it had been cut down just weeks after the picture was taken to allow wider shoulders along the road to make it safer for drivers. Coral studied the newspaper story. It was a picture of her dangling from the tree much like a teddy bear hanging from a roadside cross. The article quoted Coral as saying she wanted to change things, make a difference, and save the environment. "It may only be a eucalypt, a single gum tree, but it is a living thing just the same and deserves respect, and respect for the animals that live in it." Coral didn't mention the Irish joke, or why the tree made her laugh. She found a pair of scissors and cut the picture out.

Postal Courier decals were stuck to her van, probably part of the paint-work by now she guessed. Coral didn't think she could afford to renew the van's registration. She was out of work, and with bugger-all prospects on the horizon. She could sell a few things to raise money, things such as the climbing spurs; after all, she won't need them again. Her tree climbing adventures were over, gone along with the tree. There was also the gnome sat beside her front door – monstrous thing – scare burglars if they came to the house.

"No one would be crazy enough to buy a four-foot tall garden gnome...except me," she chortled. She put the newspaper clipping under a Humphrey B. Bear magnet on the fridge door.

Coral reached for a Tupperware container and heard foil packets rattle at the back of the shelf. She pulled them down, two packs of oxycodone hydrochloride, five milligrams each. She'd almost forgotten they were there. Doctor Drysdale had prescribed them when the pain in her foot was not responding to non-narcotic analgesics. She didn't take them – suffered the pain – just put the pills away.

"Put them away for a rainy day," Coral declared to a dazzling square of sunlight on the linoleum floor. "A day like today," she added bitterly. She pressed her fingernails under the lip of the container.

Coral had worked at the depot alongside men, tough, quick to anger men. When they argued and fought over space in the shed, Coral worked outside. On those days when rain flooded the loading area, Coral threw plastic tarpaulins over her van and worked on. In winter when her back ached from carrying boxes of wine, and car tyres, she kept it to herself. She could lift as much as any of them.

When Drysdale told her tests for cancer came back positive, she refused to believe it. She vowed to keep it to herself – ignore it and pretend it never happened. But Coral couldn't hide her illness for long. She caught the sneaking glances, the head shaking. She imagined they felt for her, felt she was a goner that is.

"Good on yer, Coral," some of the men would call out as she walked through the shed on her way to the office. She told them if any offered to help she would knock their block off. In the end, though, she took their help. They were hard but good blokes. When the cancer had gone and she broke her foot, she was tired of the routine, the side effects of one medicine piled onto another. She twisted the foil-sealed packets about her fingers.

Tobacco in the Tupperware container had not gone off; it smelt strong and pungent – made her giddy – hadn't smelled Champion Ruby Ready Rubbed since giving up. It took cancer to make her give up cigarettes. She pulled a bottle of rum out of the fridge and rolled a smoke. The tobacco assaulted her lungs, made her cough. She steadied herself by throwing back the rum – warm, intoxicating, blissfully relaxing. Coral's attention once more drifted to the newspaper photo clipped to the fridge. It showed her squeezed between the harness straps attached to climbing gear. Fatigue cramped her legs and she gave up holding her weight against the spurs, instead dangled helplessly in the harness.

Coral laughed, then cried, then laughed again through tears. She recalled the moment – didn't know if it was the worst moment in her life or the best. She didn't want the effort of remembering bad things, especially when she was hanging from a large tree beside a road. "Focus," she reminded herself, "always on the good."

Coral recalled listening to the early morning news presenter on local radio a day after her rescue, saying, "A local woman has gone to extraordinary lengths in tying a banner to the top of a tree in an attempt to save it from removal."

She hadn't counted on getting stuck up the tree, and plan B was not going well. Plan B was to call for help, but when she tried to reach her phone the lanyard slipped, and she dare not let go of her grip on the thick rope stuck around the massive trunk.

For fifteen years Coral drove past the tree she now clung to – clung to it as she had clung to the fat, useless pillock she'd been married to, before she kicked him out. She worked the beat out to the Heads and up to Berry delivering parcels and Express Post. She had worn-out three vans, survived cancer, and a broken foot.

The cancer was nothing, really. It was the treatment that almost did her in. The chemo made her crook – she lost her hair, wore a beanie all summer and looked like shit. Coral had the contract for towns along the Sand Track. The Sand Track wound its way from the river, hugging the coastline till it joined the highway further north. It was a short cut used by locals. But more and more tourists used the road to escape congestion on the highway during peak season. No sick pay when you're out there on your own, self-employed like that. She couldn't trust the job to anyone else – worked on through the sickness and pain. The Bum Tree grew beside the Sand Track and it kept her going. A wicked growth at the base of the tree looked like a well-endowed bottom poking up out of the ground. She laughed every time she saw it. Silly, really.

"Why did the Irishman bury his wife with her bum in the air? He wanted somewhere to park his bicycle," she could hear Billy shouting. She fancied Billy Connelly when she was a young strapper. His joke made her laugh when the chemo just made her puke.

When Coral hurt her foot, she went to see if it was serious. Drysdale was old school, dour and businesslike, and never laughed or joked like younger Doctors at the practice. Drysdale said her foot was broken. When asked how she did it, she told her the truth – dropped a gnome on it. She caught a flicker of amusement on her GP's face. Coral went back to work after a couple of days. The men at the depot laughed upon hearing her story – funniest story ever. Coral laughed too, saw the funny side of it. But the pain did not go away. Drysdale told her she needed to rest her foot, rest it for three months or she would run the risk of losing it altogether.

When Coral returned to the depot after three months her job had gone. Her contract had been re-negotiated. The mail never stops, Coral knew that much. It was the very notion that kept her committed to the job, the challenge, the do or die attitude of the drivers she worked with. Coral did her duty through flooded causeways and bush fires. She navigated her delivery van beneath wild winds that snapped tree tops and speared branches into the road, and now she was tossed aside. She felt bitter and abandoned, as withered as service station carnations for sale by a petrol pump.

"Damned if I will lose this one," Coral declared upon hearing the fate of the Bum Tree – her tree.

She found the second hand climbing spurs advertised for auction online. Coral had no liking for climbing trees – events collided that's all. Coral hoped they were put up for sale by a retired arborist eager to give tips on how to use them. But the young woman selling had no interest in the equipment, except to declare it belonged to her ex, and she wanted it gone. Looking at the harness and array of carbineers, helmets and knee pads splattered across the yard made Corel uncomfortable. It looked to be the aftermath of a horrible accident – former owner fell out of tree – gear bought as is where is.

"Silly cow," Coral chided herself as she loaded the bits and pieces into her van. She no longer clung to wild notions and unwavering belief that anything was possible. "Too bloody old for that." Coral slumped against the door of her van. She recalled the delicious excitement of her youth, the growing awareness of being wanted. She loved the burning sand when it squelched between her toes, running for relief from spreading water, and flaunting along the creeping waves, careless of looks and sun-ray damage. She was fearless, invincible – capable of dishing out as good as she got. She hung the helmet from the cargo barrier by its chin strap.

"Is it such a nonsense to try and save something that lived before I did?" Coral slammed the van door. "A tree living long after I've gone..." the words sounded peculiar, even as she said it. She had not thought about going, the end, not thought about it in a stark, confronting way.

Coral found a video clip on You Tube featuring a

young bit of crumpet with an English accent, who advised her to adjust the lanyard to lean out at roughly forty five degrees. If the climber is too close the spurs may slip. The man promised it was easy to climb a tree – a couple of steps, flick the lanyard, and take a couple more. Coral climbed an old Jacaranda in the back yard for a bit of practise – clambered up actually – grazed her thighs.

"Hello." A voice came from beneath her. Coral had not heard the car pull up. A young woman wearing a sleeveless cardigan and denim shorts looked up, watched her dangle in the air. "Do you need help?" She asked.

No, I'm making a stinking fool of myself without your help, thanks anyway, Coral thought, wanting to slap her.

"Yes, Yes." Coral croaked miserably. The young woman pulled out her phone and took pictures.

Coral laughed at the newspaper clipping, laughed until it hurt. She took a puff, squinted when smoke went into her eye. She popped one of the pills from the foil pack and washed it down with the rum – the familiar fug in her kitchen – sunlight streaming in smoke.

"Good thing you didn't lose bladder control up there girlie," Coral said, gazing at her picture from the newspaper. She found it hard to focus, hard to stay awake. "How many rounds is it," she wondered, "till the fighter throws in the towel? Or maybe the bloody thing's thrown in for them." She felt herself fall forward against the cold enamel of the refrigerator as she fumbled another pill from the packet. But it slipped from her numb fingers and hit the floor with a pleasant chink.

About the author:
Athol Henry lives beside the Pumicestone Passage in south east Queensland, Australia. He has had several stories published in various anthologies of short stories.

Small Miracles

Tracy Fells

Maria waited for me outside the church hall, huddled against the redbrick wall, hunched and hidden within her fur-lined hood. My breath hung in the air like lazy mist. "You can wait inside the church – the main chapel door is always unlocked," I said, fumbling the key into the ice-glazed lock.

Inside Maria trudged behind, following me all the way to my office. Papers and books lay across the desk where I had been working late the night before on my sermon for the Christmas mass.

"Don't you worry about vandals?" said Maria.

I tried to smile but my teeth felt more inclined to chatter; the air temperature had dived into minus numbers that morning. "I believe a church should be freely accessible to anyone and everyone. Sanctuary for those who need it."

Maria kept her hood up concealing one half of her pale face.

"If I show you where it's stored then could you set up the nativity crib," I said, half-turning towards the doorway leading to my office. "Otherwise a usual vacuum round will do." The Eskimo hood nodded back at me.

After a second cup of black coffee, more sugar than coffee, my headache began a strategic retreat. I rubbed the absence of sleep from my eyes. Maria was squirting the baby Jesus with cleaning fluid. The other carved figures of the nativity scene, now smelling of sharp lemons, were lined up patiently waiting to be assigned their places in the crib. I thought Maria would enjoy this task, but she performed her work with solemn concentration.

I missed the usual background soundtrack of her girlish voice, as she chattered on about Dave, her boyfriend, and his mates in the dockyard.

"Father Benedict?"

I hoped for an easy question.

"Abortion is a sin, isn't it, according to the Catholic Church?"

Glancing upwards to St. Mary's famous marble Christ, poised above the central altar, I sought guidance. Most of my parishioners were living on the wrong side of seventy so the subject of abortion rarely came up in conversation. Maria's question made me fidget with my collar. "Abortion is not sanctioned by the Holy Father." Despite my lack of confidence with this topic I tried to answer her truthfully. "All life is sacred and beloved by Jesus Christ, but…" I faltered.

"What do *you* believe, Father Benedict?"

I couldn't answer because I didn't know what I believed anymore.

Her hood slipped back and she quickly pulled it up again. Briefly I glimpsed the purple weal splattered across her cheek. Maria's eyes, flitting like a nervous bird, met mine and she stated, "I slipped on some ice."

"You need to be careful," I said. "Please look after yourself, Maria." Whose anger had whipped against her flesh? Dave – the boyfriend? Her father? Again my gaze skipped up to the crucifixion effigy. I would pray for her later, as someone clearly needed to look after this girl.

She followed my stare. "Gran says religion is all smoke and mirrors. The Church parades Jesus like a pantomime horse. Blood of Christ and all that rubbish is just Valium for the oldies – everything you do and say is an illusion. It's not real."

"Perhaps you should bring your gran along to the

midnight mass on Christmas Eve," I replied. "St. Mary's is a special place. During the war this area of the city was badly bombed, being so close to the docks, yet this church remained intact, never hit. The locals gathered here for safety and during one heavy raid," I paused to ensure she was still listening, "the statue was seen to weep real tears."

Maria snorted and turned back to the crib. "Smoke and mirrors," she mumbled.

It was past eleven and once again I was alone, working in my office next to the hall. The words for my sermon skulked in the shadows, teasing and taunting me. Another sleepless night loomed. What comfort could I bring to a world where pregnant teenagers were beaten and bruised?

As I packed away my books I saw a light within the church. Certain I'd turned off the central switch hours ago I went to investigate. In front of Christ's statue stood a large woman. Late fifties with a tight peroxide perm she swung her bulk round to face me. Her cheeks and throat were crimson, rolls of fat hung from her neck like the bulbous vocal sac of a bullfrog. In her taut features I recognised a glimmer of Maria, St. Mary's cleaner. This monstrous creation was Maria's grandmother.

"You've filled her head with sanctimonious crap." She launched her attack without an introduction. Her voice screeched at me. "Now she wants to keep the baby! I'm not raising another bastard in my house. Her mother was just fifteen when she had Maria and then scarpered leaving me with the kid." A chubby finger leapt forward to curse me. "Stay away from Maria. Or next time this will be yours!"

The woman carried a white plastic tub. Dark wine-red liquid splashed onto St. Mary's Christ, across his protruded ribs, up his neck, and a trail of red dots lashed his carved face like a whip. It was paint, not blood, but I understood the threat.

With her business concluded the woman shuffled up the nave towards the church doors. I watched her leave without comment, my hands shaking.

The following Friday morning Maria didn't turn up for work. Snow had been forecast for later that afternoon. It was Christmas Eve and I flitted like a restless sparrow, trimming candles and constantly re-posing the crib figures. One particular donkey, with only three legs, refused to stand upright so I tried to prop it against a kneeling shepherd. Toppling over for the third time I was ready to hurl the blessed creature against the stone pillar.

From behind came a cough. I spun round quickly.

A young lad stood beside Maria. His top lip was cut and swollen, his left arm encased in plaster and covered by a linen sling, stained and torn. "This is Dave," said Maria.

Maria's facial bruise had faded, but now her right eye was swollen shut.

"Oh dear," I offered, employing my "I'm only a simple Priest" tone, "did you also slip on some ice?" Dave nodded. "Perhaps you should get onto the council," I added with the hint of a smile.

Dave concentrated on his trainers, avoiding my gaze.

Maria put one hand to her belly. "We need your help Father Benedict."

I sat them both down in the front row of the pews. "What can I do?" What could an insomniac priest without sufficient patience to balance a wooden donkey offer these poor children?

"Dave and I want to have the baby," she began, "and we're going to get married too. But Gran doesn't approve…"

An understatement, I guessed.

"Maria can't stay at home anymore, Father," Dave added. "And her gran knows where I live too. We were hoping you would know somewhere, some place safe, where Maria could go. Just till we get sorted."

"Dave's got a full apprenticeship at the dockyard," said Maria with pride.

I could have lectured them about the order of their key life events, the need for restraint before wedlock, and all that rubbish. But with dwindling attendance at weekly services, and the reality that my faith seemed fit only to serve those passing time in God's waiting room, then who was I to chastise the innocent with fragile boundaries.

"Okay," I said. "I may know of a place that could help Maria." With only hours to spare before the busiest night of my year I should have chased them off with a telephone number, but they had come to me.

I drove them both to a local women's hostel – a safe harbour for those seeking sanctuary from violence, though typically the danger usually came from the woman's male partner not the maternal grandmother.

A tepid Surrey upbringing hadn't prepared me for this landscape. In my cosseted, but lonely, existence I had once believed the blessed Madonna brought only love and light to the shadows. Now I depended on prescription medicines, and a dash of Irish, to pluck up the courage to close my eyes at night.

The sound of the foghorn was muffled, like the garbled eery cry of a sea monster, in the early morning freezing fog. The light was on again inside the church, just as the telephone caller had described. "Thought you'd want to know Father – 'specially after the other attack..." The incident with the red paint had been attributed to vandals, and I fed the rumours unable to risk any comeback to Maria.

It was the first day of the New Year. The church doors were unlocked, as always, and I pushed them open.

Inside I felt the quiet of the dead, the stillness that surrounds an open casket propped in the nave.

She must have died hours before, as her body was already stiff. Her eyes were open, dilated pupils staring into nothing. The pool of ruby-red had congealed almost to a crust where it seeped across the stone floor.

From the angle of her neck and body I guessed that Maria's gran had fallen back against the stone column, the back of her head slamming into the crenelated stonework smashing open her skull.

Beside her lay Christ on his cross, the object of her destruction. Somehow the marble stature must have come loose and fallen onto the woman knocking her backwards against the column. Kneeling I reached out to touch the smooth, polished face of Christ, in my sleep deprived state I could've sworn it was wet.

Maria's grandmother had returned to St. Mary's with who knows what intent – to search out Maria perhaps, or simply to play out her malicious threat? Bizarrely, her prophetic words had come true and this time blood had been spilled.

The weekly Evening Herald's headline succinctly summed up the incident at St. Mary's: "Death in the church – a tragic accident". The blurb recounted how St. Mary's had recently been targeted by vandals and speculated that such intruders could have tampered with the hanging of the hand-carved statue, causing the massive piece of marble to topple onto the woman.

It was a good story, almost gothic, but all conjecture of

course. There was no real proof or evidence to back it up. Yet, I didn't offer any alternative explanation for the accident. After the paint attack I had supervised the cleaning of the statue, which involved unhooking the figure and bringing it down to earth. I also closely monitored its re-hanging and thoroughly checked the tightness and solidity of the screws and wires that held the cross in place. All had been quite secure and safe.

Was I, as Maria accused, simply a peddler of quack sentiments, a master of illusion fooling my feeble-minded parishioners with a steady drip-feed of magic tricks? I had to believe that God had his reasons for the woman's death. I had to believe something.

Almost a year on I was again preparing to deliver my sermon for the Christmas Eve mass. There was a good turnout – demonstrating that notoriety can do wonders for attendance ratings.

In the pulpit I stood invigorated, ready to share my aspirations, hopes and beliefs with my congregation. The return of a good night's sleep has helped. I swear that hot milk and renewed faith were more effective than drugs. My faith now resided in those before me.

Two faces watched me as I spoke. Maria and her husband Dave had come as promised and Ben, their son, slept in his mother's arms. Maria had been blessed with a healthy baby, and I could vouch for the power of his lungs from the christening service. The parents were young, simple in their wants and outlook, but they loved their child and each other. Small miracles in a troubled world, but I clung to whatever debris of hope He tossed me.

With palms outstretched I blessed their future while a contented smile settled on my lips. I could live with small miracles.

About the author:
Tracy Fells has won and been placed in numerous competitions for fiction and drama. She was shortlisted for the 2014 Commonwealth Writers Short Story Prize. Her short stories and flash fiction are published online, in anthologies and in national magazines. Currently she is working on a novel and an MA in Creative Writing at Chichester University. She shares a blog with The Literary Pig (http://tracyfells.blogspot.co.uk) and tweets as @theliterarypig.

Someone like You

William Wilson

1

When I saw him he was standing smack in the middle of the grand foyer of The Plaza, shoulders hunched like a bear as he tapped on his Blackberry. Other hotel guests, celebrities, politicians, high class call girls, bellboys and porters jostled round him like flotsam swirling round a rock. It was five years since I'd last seen him. He looked up from his phone, raised a hand to stop my advance.

"Just a minute," he said, and finished his email, then threw a heavy arm around my shoulders.

"Phil, thanks for coming old mate."

His accent had changed, now a strange mix of Scottish and South African, but you still had to wait for him to finish whatever he was doing before you got his attention and then the same affectionate familiarity. He looked tanned and prosperous but different somehow, older.

"Thanks for inviting me." I responded.

His big frame was bunched up in a coat.

"I thought we were eating here," I said, "Are we going out?"

"They're keeping me a table here, but I thought we could have a walk before dinner. Is that OK? I need some air."

We headed across the road and down the steps to the beach. It was cold and starting to rain. Hunched up against the wind and with the sea crashing over the shingle it was difficult to hear each other speak. He was staying at The Plaza overnight, thought he'd "look up an old mate."

I let his bonhomie wash over me. Living on my own

141

and short of company I'd jumped at the chance of re-living the good times, even if only for an evening. Campbell and I had worked together for nearly twenty years back in the '70s and '80s. I'd had to save his skin on many an occasion.

We had reached the steps by the pier.

"Come on," he said, "let's get out of the rain. I could do with a drink." And he hustled us along the boardwalk and into a great barn of a place, strobing lights, a smell of beer, sweat, cheap perfume.

"Hey, this is something, isn't it?" he shouted above the noise.

A fat blond woman in gold heels and a shiny red evening dress was crooning lustily into the microphone. Sweat stained her armpits.

Campbell banged me on the back. "What's your poison nowadays? Don't tell me it's still Campari soda."

"I'll have a small lager thanks."

The carpets stank. Campbell ordered a pint and a whisky chaser for himself. He'd commandeered a small table beside the stage steps. He took off his coat to reveal a fine Italian suit, crisp white shirt open at the neck, gold cufflinks. His shaved head glistened beneath the disco lights. He gulped back his beer. His bulk swamped the chair as he leaned backwards to take in the stage. The fat woman had removed her dress to loud jeers revealing lacy underwear and fishnet tights. As she left the stage Campbell grabbed one cheek of her backside. She gave a little gasp, looked down at him, liked what she saw.

"Wanna buy me a drink sweetheart?" She was leaning over our table, but with one eye on a paunchy slit eyed man with a red neck and lumberjack shirt who was advancing towards Campbell.

"Sorry darling: not tonight." Campbell stood up

142

slowly, gathered his coat and raised a warning hand towards the advancing threat.

"We're leaving sonny. Don't start something you can't finish." He bent down to pick up his whisky, and deliberately took his time drinking it, all the while staring down the man with the red neck. Campbell could be intimidating when he wanted to be. The fine clothes didn't hide the great barrel chest straining under the white shirt. He had no neck, just folds of muscle under the bald head which looked as if it had been hammered down into his shoulders. His eyes were merciless. The red necked man had stopped and stood leaning forward, trying to look aggressive, but his face was pallid and he was looking anywhere except at my companion. When Campbell pushed me towards the door and bludgeoned his way past him, he stepped aside.

2

Heading back to the hotel in the rain Campbell had his arm round my shoulder shouting into my ear. "You've got it all here, haven't you?"

"What do you mean?"

"What about the women in that bar?"

"Not the sort of place I go: surely you've got that in South Africa."

"Not white women like that, Phil, only black."

He was clearly excited. I didn't know how to respond.

Back at The Plaza the doorman saluted Campbell in his cashmere coat and ignored me in my mackintosh as we revolved through the doors. Leaving our coats at the desk Campbell headed for the bar.

"I need a proper drink," he said, "before we eat.

What'll you have? Come on, not another bloody lager. I'm having a Pernod."

I hesitated, "Campbell, it's very kind, I don't drink much..." but before I had got the words out he had said, "Barman, make that two."

The Pernod arrived, cloudy with iced water. In spite of my reservations I revelled in the sweet cold shock of it.

"Here's to you Campbell. Thanks for inviting me. You look to be doing very well for yourself."

He shrugged. "You never know what's round the corner. And how are you Phil? I was sorry to hear about Elaine. How long ago...?" His voice trailed away.

"Four years next month."

"You didn't have children did you?"

"No."

"And you're living near here?"

"Yeah, I've a flat further down the seafront."

I didn't want to talk about me.

"How's Katie and the boys?" I said.

"They're all good thanks."

The boys were away at university, one at Harvard, one at Oxford. He went on to tell me about the house near Cape Town, three storeys overlooking the ocean.

"There's a private pathway to the beach," he said. "It's quite isolated. We have to have a 24 hour armed guard, mainly for Katie's sake," he added. "I'm away a lot."

"I don't know how you keep it up."

He shrugged again. "I suppose you think I should just retire to a little flat by the seaside, do you?"

I should have been hurt, but this was typical of his manner. The pain must have shown in my face for immediately he'd stretched out a hand, taken my arm, looked directly into my eyes, and apologised.

"Sorry mate, take no notice, I'm not really myself. I care about you, you know. I remember the good times. Come on, let's have another Pernod and then go and eat."

I let it pass.

The maitre d' had saved Campbell a table by the window. I wondered how he could command this level of service, how he had become so formidable. He was a bull dressed in haute-couture. Everything about him was immaculately laundered, pressed, shaped, polished, and when we sat down to the meal he put on his happy face, leaning back and throwing an arm over the chair back, a hand pulling on his chin, or his head right down and his dark shiny eyes looking up, eyebrows raised, the skin rippling upwards on his forehead as he looked at the menu. He raised a finger to summon the waiter. He was irrepressible, ordering oysters and a bottle of stout followed by steak and a bottle of claret.

"You can't just have grilled fish," he said as I ordered. "At least have some oysters to start."

"No Campbell. You have them and enjoy them. I'm quite happy to sit here and keep you company."

"What wine will you have?" he asked me as the sommelier hovered.

"Just a glass of white, thanks."

"What? You're a different man to the one I knew. Look, they do a lovely chablis. Have a carafe."

"OK, the chablis, but just a glass," I insisted, "Oh, and a glass of water."

"Tap water, sir?"

"Yes please."

"With ice and lemon Sir?" There was the merest trace of a smirk.

"No thanks."

145

The sommelier turned to go, but Campbell had crooked his finger to lasso him back to the table.

"Are you trying to be funny, Laddie?" he said.

The sommelier's face had gone white: "No, Sir. Sorry, Sir." He scraped his way backwards and escaped toward the kitchen.

"D'yr remember that slimy waiter in Venice? Insisting that spaghetti vongele didn't need garlic?" Cambell's voice was becoming a bit slurred.

"Oh yeah, and Fergus insisted it did," I said,

"And Peter got into a fight with the chef..."

"Was that the same trip we'd eaten all those olives and the chewed stones were in that bowl and then Linda, you know Linda from PR, tried to eat them thinking they were pistachios?"

And so on. The conversation was moving onto familiar ground, a long succession of foreign conferences and meetings, airports and hotels, restaurants and bars. Campbell became more maudlin as he became more mellow.

"I dunno what we'd have done without you, you know." He was deep in memory, shaking his head. "You kept us legal. We would have been in a terrible mess. D'you know what we used to call you?"

"You've told me before. You called me the golden shovel."

"Yeah, I've never seen so much shit cleared up so elegantly."

"You're too kind." I said.

"No, I mean it. I always felt as if I could sleep at night so long as you were looking after things. I could always rely on you."

He could too. I'd given him his first job, promoted him, watched his star rise in the firmament, basked in his light and watched his back. He now inhabited a world beyond my reach.

I was brought back to the present by the waiter.

"Let me do that for you Sir," flicking open a napkin; "Is the steak to Sir's liking?"

"Would you like a little more béarnaise sauce, Sir?"

"More wine Sir?"

I felt we were under acute observation all the time.

"But everything's under control now, isn't it?" I asked.

"Christ, yes."

"And business is good?"

"You could say that," he grinned.

The dessert had arrived, and with it the first hint of why Campbell was so much the centre of attention.

"And you've now set up the Cape Development group, is that right? I saw an interview with you on Bloomberg, and there was that feature in Time magazine."

"Yeah, things are going really well. Between you and me I was lucky with the timing."

"So Campbell," I paused to get his attention, and he looked up from his crepes suzette, "are you going to tell me what brings you to Brighton?"

He grinned. "I thought you'd never ask." He waved his fork vaguely around the room. "This."

"What do you mean, this? The restaurant? No, surely not."

"Philip, Philip," he sighed. "Not the restaurant, the hotel."

"What do you mean, the hotel. It's long past its best."

"I've just bought it," he smiled.

"You've bought it?" I echoed.

"Well, Cape Development Group has." He grinned again. "It's a bit of a dump, isn't it, this place, begging for re-development. I closed the deal on Monday. Most of the staff know. There'll be an official announcement tomorrow."

3

We ordered coffee. He'd gone quiet. He looked up at me a few times. Something was coming, I could tell.

"When did you retire, Phil?"

"I took voluntary redundancy, if that's what you mean. About twelve years ago. We had enough to live on and I wanted to look after Elaine."

"And you haven't worked since?"

"What could I do? The old firm had gone. I didn't want all the hassle of running another organisation."

He thought for a minute and then said, "I could use someone like you now." It was as if the words had been dropped into a pond. Surely he wasn't offering me a job? My heart jumped and fluttered. I could have done with a bit of additional income but not a full time job again. I felt my way forward, like a blind man reaching for a chair.

"Do you mean, back in South Africa?"

"Not necessarily."

"And when you say, 'someone like me,' what do you mean?"

"Someone I can trust."

I waited for him to go on, but then, suddenly cutting off the flow, he said, "Shall we have a brandy, or perhaps a port?" He picked up the wine list.

"Not for me thanks. I've had quite a lot already. I need to be careful."

"Careful? What for? You've no-one else to worry about?"

He'd done it again. As soon as the words were out he was apologising. He reached forward out of his seat and put a hand on my shoulder and I shrugged it off. He wafted the waiter away.

"I've had enough of this place. Let's go out and find somewhere more lively." Before I could protest he had pushed back his chair, got to his feet somewhat unsteadily, chucked his napkin on the table, and waded through a small gaggle of anxious waiters towards the concierge to collect our coats.

"Are you sure about this Campbell?" I asked. "Most of the places around here are a bit noisy, a bit sleazy."

"That's fine by me. Where'll we go?"

"I've no idea. I don't do this sort of thing any longer."

"Come on man, it's still early. We'll find somewhere to have a drink, then you can come back to the hotel if you like. There'll be a room going spare."

So, against my better judgement, we went back out into the night and headed towards West Street. Thank goodness it had stopped raining, but it was still cold and the pavements were black and slippery, water everywhere. Large groups of youths were swaggering down the street, many already drunk, the girls with hardly anything on in spite of the cold. There were queues around cash machines, and longer queues waiting for admission to bars and clubs. It was obvious nowhere here was going to let us past the door, we were over twice the maximum age everywhere we looked. We got trapped in a passageway by a police patrol called to break up a fight. A pair of club bouncers were attacking a youth spread-eagled on the ground, a jeering crowd looking on. Finally the police let us through and we found a place near the Pavilion. It was a pub rather than a club, all deep red and yellow ochre, a copper panelled ceiling, ornate mirrors and chandeliers, giant fans. The place seemed full of foreign students and Campbell lurched through them, swaying towards the bar.

149

You couldn't hear yourself speak. There was nowhere to sit. Campbell bought beers and whiskies for the two of us, balancing them on the top of a slot machine. I was annoyed, but puzzled also.

I sipped at my beer, and pushed my whisky away. "You have it." I said, and he just chucked it down his throat. He had always been a hard drinker but never an unwise one. I'd never known him lose control so completely. I started to wonder if something was going badly wrong in his life. He seemed intent on destroying himself.

There was a group of students near us, kids really, pushing and giggling, beers in their hands, intent it seemed on pouring the dregs from a glass over the head of one of their number. The group swayed this way and that. Someone tripped pulling down two or three others after him. A girl fell backwards into Campbell who caught her round her bare midriff and then wouldn't let her go. She squirmed, bit his arm, and he jerked back, knocking our drinks over. There were shards of glass and pools of beer all over the floor. Two burly men advanced towards the group amid a general scramble to escape. I pulled Campbell towards the door and we crashed through it in a jumble of arms and legs, Campbell sprawling heavily across the kerb, half in the gutter. It had started raining again, water pouring out of a broken drainpipe across the pavement where Campbell lay. I tried to pull him upright, but he couldn't get up straightaway. When he did he bent over, one arm still hanging onto me and was violently sick. I felt that was probably a good thing. I tried to lead him away from the mess on the pavement and towards the seafront in the hope of finding a taxi. There was no hope of getting him back to The Plaza on foot, even if it were only a few hundred yards away.

"Good man, Philip." He was slurring. "Good man, remember that time you saved me in Berlin, I still owe you mate." Then, a little later. "And what about that bar, the Blue Moon, in New York. What a shithole," and so on. The awful thing was that I did remember, and in amongst all the squalid details, I couldn't help being excited. Meanwhile, Campbell was in a dreadful state, his cashmere coat sodden right through, vomit over his shoes and ankles, a knee showing through a rip in his trousers. But on the seafront, there was a taxi just dropping a party off. I helped Campbell into the back before the driver could object and with some embarrassment asked for The Plaza.

Even as the cabbie was pointing out The Plaza was but a short walk, Campbell regained his senses enough to intervene.

"No Philip, no. Not The Plaza. Not like this."

"Come on Campbell, we've got to get you out of these clothes and cleaned up and warm."

"Phil," he paused, "mate." He paused again. I knew what was coming. "Can we go to yours? Do you mind… save me again, just this once. We need to talk. I've got to talk to you. It's important."

I had no idea what he was saying, he was too far gone. But I had to admit that if he really was the new owner of The Plaza he couldn't be seen there in that state.

"All right." Wearily I turned to the cabbie. "Porchester Court. Far end of Hove Lawns"

4

I'd sold the house and moved into Porchester Court after Elaine died. I loved the flat, its elegant rooms overlooking the sea on one side and the lawns on the other. I loved the entrance with the smart letter boxes and bell pushes, the

151

brass handles and marbled hallways, and the wood panelled lifts which reminded me of old department stores.

I lived on the third floor. It had been a struggle getting Campbell safely to my door. He threw up again, but it was whilst we were still outside, thank goodness. I had to go down later with a mop and bucket and hoped no-one was looking. He was dripping wet, leaving a trail of water along the hallway and muddy puddles in the lift. He was murmuring all the time, variations on, "You're a good man, Phil. Dunno what I'd have done without you." I dragged him into the bathroom and sat him on the toilet seat, then helped him off with his shoes and most of his clothes.

I knew that I should try and keep him awake and sitting up and warm, so I wrapped him in a towelling robe I used for the beach, the only garment I had which he could get into. I helped him into the lounge and guided him to an armchair near the fire. I went to the kitchen to get the washing-up bowl – I couldn't risk him being sick on my carpet – and gave him a big glass of water which he put down with a grimace.

"You're not getting anything else. And don't keep thanking me." I said before he had a chance to thank me again.

It got quite late and his condition seemed to stabilise. I'd put on the television news to help keep him occupied, but he asked me to switch it off.

"There's something I must tell you," he said.

"Not now Campbell. Look, I think we can get you to bed now. We can talk in the morning."

"No, I must tell you now," he said, "I've been wanting to all evening." He sighed. "We can talk more in the morning but I must tell you now." His voice was heavy, but with something more than drink.

"Go on," I said.

"I didn't really come to Brighton to go to The Plaza. I came to see you."

"Me?" I couldn't understand what he was leading up to. "You came all this way to see me?" I repeated.

He was peering at me through half closed eyes, looking for help. "I'm dying, Phil."

I was completely shocked, frozen to the chair. I must have been gaping at him. I waited.

He was in a fog and struggling to be clear of it. "I've seen all the best doctors, had all the tests. I got the final results in London this week. I've got a tumour on my brain. They can't operate."

I let the silence settle, leaned forward and put a hand on his arm. "Does Katie know?"

He took a big intake of breath, looked at me and shook his head. "No-one knows, Phil. No-one. Only you."

He looked immensely weary. "I need your help."

I could see his eyelids beginning to close. I helped him to his feet and led him to the spare bedroom. "We'll talk in the morning."

5

I slept fitfully. I'd misread the signs the previous evening, the dropped hints, the reckless behaviour. Campbell probably slept like a child. He was still sleeping long after I was up and breakfasted. I wondered if he might have had any appointments. He'd said there would be an announcement about the ownership of The Plaza tomorrow and I rang them so they knew where he was.

He came into the kitchen, still wearing my towelling robe and looking grey and haggard.

"Thanks for saving me last night." His voice was weak.

153

"Do you want a coffee?" I asked.

"Coffee? Yeah."

"Anything to eat." I had a sudden inspiration. "I could do you some porridge."

"Porridge?" He laughed, shook his head as if in disbelief, looked up at me. "The real thing? Then yes."

He sat by the window looking out to sea whilst I prepared the oats. I wondered how much he remembered about the previous evening.

"You said some pretty serious things last night." I said,

"I told you about the tumour, didn't I?"

"Yes." I paused, "You said you're dying."

"I am, Phil. They can't operate."

"Yes, you said last night."

"I get these terrible headaches. They say they're just the start. And I get so tired, you can't bloody believe it. Some days it's OK, like yesterday, but other days I get so weary. All I want to do is sleep. It'll get worse and worse, and more frequent."

"And do you know how long...?" I forced myself to look at him.

"A few months." He started to become more matter-of-fact. "I need help, Phil. Will you help me?"

"If I can, yes of course, but I don't see how. Don't you need to be back home, back with your family? You need them surely, not someone like me?"

"You're right, I do, but I need to sort a few things out before I see them." He explained he'd had a new will drawn up by lawyers in London. There was a draft copy in the room-safe in the hotel. Would I be one of the executors?

"I can trust you Phil. You're one of the only people I know I can trust. You'd be well compensated by the way.

154

It's all provided for."

I said I would. I was flattered. It was something I could do, and I genuinely wanted to help.

"I want to read it first." I said.

"Of course." He said. "Good old Phil. Cautious to the end." But there was more to come, I could tell. He inched towards it.

"Phil, can I ask you? I don't recall you're being especially religious?"

"Not at all." But where was this leading?

"You know about 'living wills'?"

"I think so, something about not being resuscitated?"

"Sort of. It's to specify how you want to be treated if you're no longer of sound mind to make any decisions. It's called an 'Advance Statement'. I've had one prepared. It needs witnessing."

"Campbell, I can't be involved in determining what treatment you receive. It's nothing to do with me. It's for you or your family to decide."

"No, no you don't understand. You wouldn't be involved in any decisions at all. I just need someone to witness my signature, that's all. Someone I can trust." There was that word again.

"OK. And this document's also at the hotel?"

"Yep."

And still there was something else. He stood up and turned to gaze at the sea, leaning forwards, hands on the windowsill. I could see him holding his breath, then, still looking straight ahead, his shoulders sagging. "There's a doctor in Hove, very distinguished. He advises on assisted dying, medically assisted suicide. You've heard of Dignitas?" He turned to face me.

"In Switzerland. Yes, of course, who hasn't?"

"This doctor campaigns to get medically assisted

155

suicide legalised. He runs discussion groups, and provides private advice. It's something I want to explore, but I don't want to see him on my own. I want a witness, someone who'll ask the difficult questions. I want someone not involved, someone I can trust."

"You want me to come with you to the meeting?"

He nodded, but I knew that wasn't the end of it.

"And after the meeting: what then?"

"That's the hard part, Phil," and once again he looked straight at me with those dark shiny eyes. "If I'm persuaded, and I should tell you that I'm minded to be persuaded, then I'll want someone to come to Switzerland with me."

"Bloody hell Campbell. You're not kidding are you?"

He'd moved across to where I was standing and before I could react he'd put an arm round my shoulder and then came a great bearhug, the rough towelling of the beachrobe rubbing against my cheek.

"I'm not sure it's legal," I said through a mouthful of towelling, but even as I said it I realised I hadn't said no: the legality was a complication, not a refusal."

"I've thought it all through," he released his bearhug but kept his arm round my shoulder. "We wouldn't leave from here: I'll be coming from Cape Town. We could meet in Paris."

"Hang on a minute. Isn't Dignitas in Switzerland?"

"It is. I thought we could have a day in Paris, stay overnight, probably at the Ritz, it's another of my hotels. We'll have a ball. No expense spared. We can go to Maxims, if you like, or what about Le Dome, then afterwards there's that great little bar in Montparnasse, Le Chat Noir, do you remember? Then next day go to Zurich by train – on the TGV, first class – it's a beautiful journey. One last trip, eh Phil. One last trip. Whadda you say?"

I couldn't believe this was happening. I could feel myself getting excited, becoming swept up in some great event. I had been there at the beginning for Campbell, I had played a key part in building his glittering career, and now I would be instrumental in bringing it all to an end.

"When's the meeting with the good doctor in Hove? I bet you've already set it up."

"I have yes. Tomorrow morning. 10.00am."

"Then we'd better get you some new clothes," I said. "We can't have you looking scruffy."

6

775 Great Ocean Road,
Western Cape,
South Africa.

May 6th.2013

Dear Philip,

I'm enclosing a clipping from The Cape Times of the memorial service for Campbell. It was a very moving ceremony, and I wish you could have been here to be a part of it.

I want to thank you for the part you played in helping Campbell during the past months. It was wonderful that he found someone like you to help him, someone he could trust. He spoke very highly of you, and I understand how difficult it must have been for you to handle such sensitive issues. I knew how close you had been when you were colleagues, but never expected you would play so large part in our lives as now.

You may be reassured to know that Campbell

and I said goodbye on the beach. Afterwards I stood looking at the ocean whilst he went back to the house and the taxi waiting to take him to the airport. It was our joint decision that I did not accompany him to Switzerland. You made that decision possible for us.

I'm also enclosing a copy of the burial service, and a photograph of the grave which is on a hillside overlooking the ocean near our home. You will know of course that Campbell's body was flown here from Switzerland. The burial took place after the memorial service and was attended only by the close family.

Lachlan is flying back to England next week to resume his studies at Oxford, and I plan to come out later in June to see him and also to see the lawyers in London. I'll be staying at Browns Hotel. I'll let you know my more detailed arrangements nearer the time, but hope very much to see you again during the trip. Perhaps I can come to Brighton, or is it Hove? Can you recommend a hotel?

With fondest regards,
Katie.

About the author:

William Wilson pursued a business career until 2003 when he decided to go travelling and then to take a BA Fine Art degree course. He graduated from Brighton University in 2010. After spending a few years painting he took up creative writing and is on a two-year Creative Writing Course with New Writing South. He is married, with two daughters, and lives in Hove.

Swallowed Up

James Farnham

"Don't you two get lost. I'll wait for you here," she shouted above the noise of the crowd.

"We'll try not to," her husband said and told Emily to hang on tightly as the pair of them thrust their way into the roar of the throng in the piazza.

It wasn't often that his four-year-old requested a walk, so he would make the best of it as he dived further into the turmoil of Siena's public holiday. It was a riot, wilder than the Palio.

He told Emily they were heading to one of the quieter streets that led off the far corner of the square. There he might be able to let go of Emily's hand; it was awkward walking with his left shoulder hanging down to keep hold of her hand, her tiny fingers enveloped in his. Looking down, all he could see was the straw blond crown of her head in the hole of the crowd packed closely around them. It was as if the whole city had joined a street dance.

"Keep hold Emily, you must keep hold!" he cried again, but she obviously couldn't hear above the noise; she couldn't even look up at him; the press of people was too dense.

He tried to imagine what it would be like down there; to be so small, her little head swimming in a sea of knees, the brightness of her blue eyes shut out from the sun above, caught up in the throes of a scary ride like the fair they had gone to back in England the previous week.

He knew why his wife had told them to be careful. She often referred to Emily as their "precious cargo". Her use of the phrase was a code for all that they had been through: the years of trying for their only child, the traumas of a difficult birth and now the blind obsession they had for the only offspring they would ever have, her perfect beauty and temperament. Often they felt suffocated by their luck.

He tried to work out what was happening with the crowd. At times he and Emily were hemmed in by a body of people heading towards the far side of the square and they would make a surge of progress in the right direction. But then they would be hurled off course as another knot of people swooped by the opposite way; it was a boiling river, thundering in the rapids.

The mob made a great swerve, like an eddy, and he felt Emily's hand being twisted and loosened in his. He screamed out her name again, urging her to hold on. He thought he heard her squeal above the deafening noise. Was he squeezing her hand too tightly? It was impossible to tell in the convulsion.

The crowd spun them round again and he felt Emily's hand starting to slip again from his. It was impossible to hold her without wrenching her arm from her shoulder. The flats of her fingers started sliding from his like a bar of soap. He remembered the time he was learning to climb and lost his grip, falling in fear until the rope snagged. There was no rope to snag. She was gone.

The screams of the crowd became her screams and his screams, they merged into one, it was the roar of the end of the world howling at him. She was taken.

With tears in his eyes he bellowed her name to the sky while the crowd churned him round. In his panic, everything fell silent in his mind; the noise was shut out and all he could see was a flurry of faces swirling round him in a carousel, their expressions knotted in contortion, struggling in the heaving mass. A toothless old woman in a black shawl laughed at him as they seemed to spin round together in a macabre dance; she must have thought he was joining in the fun, a tourist enjoying the mayhem.

The silence in his head ended abruptly as the shrillness of the crowd flooded back in, each shout filling his ears, but none of them were Emily's; the small flute of her voice was lost and would never be heard again.

In his loss, he wanted to collapse and fall to the ground, but because he was tall, the compression around him was pushing him upwards rather than down, the reverse of what would have happened to Emily. He tried to burrow below to howl for her among the feet that would surely have trampled her by now, the fractures of her head and her fragile bones. *Dear God, please not*, he thought, trying to sound her name, but the pressure against him meant he could barely exhale. He felt empty and hollowed out in defeat; he had betrayed her, and the trust that had been placed in him.

Surely she would be determined, as only her own poor heart could be, the way it pounded when he read her stories or played ball with her in the garden. Yes, surely she would be strong; *please be strong, stay upright and do not fall*. He willed the words and choked on them, rolling in the swell of people like waves on the sea.

Don't you two get lost.

He had to think.

He looked back to the tall clock tower behind him. He was more than half way across the square, being propelled by the crowd towards the far side. If Emily was still standing she would be caught up somewhere in the same flow. He clung to the thought that they might be spat out of the fray in the same place and at the same time.

Eventually he forced himself to the corner of the square where steps led up to the streets that branched away from the piazza. Emily was not there and he sat

161

down at the top of the steps, drained, staring down at his crossed legs with his hands wrapped over the back of his head. He didn't mind if he looked as if he was begging, because he was; pleading for Emily to appear, rocking himself pitifully.

He thought about what to do, whether to go to the police first or phone his wife, and then he remembered he had no phone or wallet; he had no need of them for such an innocent stroll and had left them behind in the rucksack.

The wrinkled old woman he had seen in the crowd was standing in front of him. He looked up. Her face was kindlier now, smiling down at him in silhouette against the sun. She seemed to be asking him whether he was all right. His Italian was poor, but he remembered the word "bambino" and held one hand above the other to convey Emily's diminutive height. He didn't know the Italian for "lost", but he remembered to use "bambina" this time, holding the flats of his hands up to the sky and knifing them apart in exasperation.

"Ah, Bambina! Bambina!" she said, gesticulating towards the street, which was busy, but not as tightly packed as the square. He leapt up, shouting "grazia" several times as he ran away in the direction she had pointed.

It made sense: Emily always listened so attentively; she would have remembered him explaining earlier where they were heading and would have run in that direction. As he ran, bumping into people, apologising as he went, he saw several children holding hands with their parents, but no children on their own.

He had gone almost a mile before he gave up, realising he should go back to his wife. The prospect of telling her what had happened filled him with dread; to cause her the same grief that he felt, the same cold sweat, even though it was hot. But then he clung to the hope that the crowd in the square might have swept Emily back to her mother, that she had been found and not led away, that she would be sitting on the pavement laughing and enjoying a gelato.

When he got back to the square, he was careful not to take the direct route back across the crowded piazza; instead he went round the edge, almost clinging to the walls, where they existed, or brushing by the people sat in the cafés. There were numerous families gabbling and enjoying themselves at the tables, which made him feel broken and empty. His arms flopped around at his side as he stumbled along, retching through his tears and barely able to stand, visualising Emily and the panic on her face when she had been trampled or abducted. *Please not*, he repeated deliriously, *please not*. He stood with his hands on his head, his eyes closed, beseeching the sky.

He was transfixed, unable to move, trying to shut out the din of the people passing by, trying to will Emily's safety and praying that the whole disaster was not real, that it had been a dream. He tried to imagine the padding of her little canvass shoes on the stone flags, a sound he had been hearing all week as Emily had rushed around in each piazza they had visited, her excited yelps echoing off the ancient walls and reverberating in the hollows of the alleys. *Please let her be safe.*

He was thinking about her so vividly that he heard her voice; he heard her still voice above the noise of the crowd. "Daddy! Daddy!" he heard, the words tripping with her feet on the pavement as fast as they could go. He opened his eyes and looked ahead, but they were dazzled from looking up at the sun, and out of focus because of his watering eyes. In the blur of the mirage he could see her running towards him, her arms outstretched, her blond hair flowing behind her, a smile filling the delight of her round face.

"Daddy! Daddy!" she said again, and he realised it was

163

real when her little fists were pummelling the front of his thighs. He pulled her up, as if drawing her out of a drowning lake. He held her high above him, up to the sun, then lowered her and buried her streaming face into his throat, their tears mingling dark on the blue of his cotton shirt.

He looked skywards again. He did not know whether the moment was damascene or an epiphany, or a salvation: he did not care. The hysteria of the crowd seemed more benign now, as if celebrating the reunion of father and daughter, their impossible renaissance.

"You let go Daddy and I got lost." Emily said.

"I know, I know," he smiled. "But you are found, you are safe."

"Yes, I'm back now."

He stood hugging her, as if he could never let go, swaying and humming a tune and then he let her down to stand again, holding her hand, tightly, even though the piazza was much less crowded now.

"Ouch, my hand," she scolded.

He held it more softly and said, "We had better go and find Mummy."

"Yes, she'll wonder where we've gone."

His wife was still sitting on the step near the clock tower where they had left her, reading her book.

"Did you two get lost?" she said.

About the author:
Before turning to creative writing, James Farnham lived on a farm in Somerset, where he ran a craft-made cider business and was involved in cheese-making. Previously he ran a business strategy and speechwriting consultancy, writing occasional features in the business press and winning the Guardian's Management Essay competition in 1999. He has recently moved to Dorset, where he is completing his first novel and experimenting with poetry and shorter forms.

The Flower Man or: Something About a Cat

Daniel Dowsing

I can't remember if it was a fox, or maybe a cat, but it darted in front of the car and now the car is on its back. A damp trickle tickles the side of my face, my head feels fat and tight as it pounds and pounds and pounds.

Katherine will be worried. Or perhaps she won't. I'm always careful, but I had a drink before I left. Or was it two?

Cold air floods through the smashed windows and I want to scratch the damp itch congealing in my hair as it drips onto the roof of the car with a

Pap

Pap

Pap

but my arms tingle with numbness.

The pounding slows, my eyes feel heavy. The dash, the wheel, the broken screen blur and pixilate. My eyes sink deeper into the darkness of my skull. Like a pendulum, my head hangs limp and long and, for a moment, I feel peaceful…

…I'm standing outside the car but it's no longer a car at all; just a crumpled mass of glass and metal like some gutted clockwork pig. Steam that should be hissing silently oozes into the air.

It's quiet; a starless night. Grey plumes of breath cloud against the darkness. Nothing tingles or stings out here;

neither cold nor pain. Street lamps reveal the odd pocket of reality but everything else is black. I must be near the park. I can see the occasional oak tree along the side of the road.

I want to look closer at the car, just a little closer, through one of the broken windows. Maybe if I crouch down, go on all fours, I'll see-

"Forgot ya then, did he?" asks a voice from the dark. "I hate it when he does that. Bloody mind fuck if yer ask me."

The man must be in his sixties. His tweed coat is buttoned up to the top. A striped blue and beige scarf fits snugly around his neck; loose jowls hang from his face. Wire-framed glasses so big they might as well be TV sets cover his eyes. Along his top lip runs the silver sliver of a moustache. Flowers wrapped in brown paper rest in his arms. White flowers. "And it means I gotta hang around here until yer picked up."

"Who are you?" I ask.

"The Flower Man," he replies.

"What're you doing here? Call an ambulance! Please! Do you have a phone? I need to call my wife! She'll be..." Out of the corner of my eye the wrecked car lingers as silent as an iceberg.

He snorts a laugh, shakes his head and brushes past me. A sign, planted in the verge, warns drivers that the next stretch of road is a winding one.

"What's a Flower Man?" I ask.

"At a push I'd say a man with flowers. Or perhaps a guy who's been doing this job for so long he's forgotten his name?... Or doesn't need a name," he replies laying the flowers at the base of the sign. A wheeze, the crumple of paper, and it's done. Just like that, without pomp or circumstance. A groan stretches out as he stands up again

166

and for a moment I imagine his joints are tattooed with rust as the white flowers lay still, dead.

I had to ask: "Are they for me?"

"Mmmhmmm" he pulls a cigarette from one pocket and a lighter from the other. Shhrrp-click-ffoom goes the lighter as his face blooms with warm, orange light and strings of curling white smoke.

The road dead ends into a wall of black and nothing. I strain my ears for something, anything I can hold onto; the sounds of distant traffic or aeroplanes in the sky. The numb air neither hot or cold. I almost believe this time and moment have been dropped into a shoe box, placed on a shelf deep down in a cellar and left to gather dust. For a second I forgot I was wearing clothes and I became an outline of air standing in the silence. Night holds its breath as we wait; this strange, old man and I on the road by the park.

"Surely it's Katherine's job to lay flowers for me?" I trail off into the silence.

"Course it is! But one day she'll forget, or stop, or whatever an' that's where I come in." He draws deep on the cigarette, sighing out torrents of smoke whilst chewing something with wet, clicking sounds.

"She wouldn't forget! It was just a stupid fight!" My arms feel tight, locked by my side. If this were a film I'd probably rough him up but instead I just stand there, like I always do, staring at the old man on the pavement; waiting for the universe to remember us.

"Oh calm down…you'll give yourself a heart attack!" He roars with laughter and for a moment I think he might slap his thigh. The laughter trails off along with his cigarette smoke, floating up and away into the sky. "Heart attack? Car crash? No? Nothing? Okay fine! She won't "forget you" forget you. Just, well, when was the las' time

167

you put flowers on your mother's grave, ay? Don't mean you've forgotten her does it."

My lips go dry at his words. Licking them doesn't help. "I think about her every day."

"Precisely. Weeping in front of stones and draping yourself across a park bench is for them Greek Tragedies – by my name those Greeks loved to mope! The only monuments that matter are here," he taps his chest. "An' out there," he twirls on the spot, arms spread like wings, cigarette fuming. "Put it this way, would you rather be reminded of her by some stuck up statue or, I don't know, the smell of her perfume? Or cigarette?"

"So you just go around putting flowers down for people you don't even know? All those flowers taped to trees and lampposts?"

"Yep. Right now there's teenage girl been knocked off a motorbike," he raises a finger on one hand. "A depressed widow hanging from a tree," a second finger. "A protest that turned violent outside Moscow and a cat who should have looked both ways before crossing the road. Want me to go on?" he says with four fingers pointing up. "Every one will get the same treatment as you." The hand returns to depths of a coat pocket.

"Why the hell would you do that?"

His face drops, eyes boring into the centre of The Earth through the grass and the rock and the roiling fires below. "Because I want to. Because they deserve it." He pauses. "Because it's a terrible thing being the first man to die."

Shattered glass twinkles on the road like a bed of fallen stars. I have no option but to wait so I sit on the kerb next to my flowers and the old man smokes his cigarette.

"You do this for cats as well?"

168

He smiles a knowing smile. "I like cats."

I sigh, driving my hands deep into my pockets hoping to feel the cold that isn't there. I scrape the soles of my feet on the loose gravel in the road just to make a noise and for a moment all I can remember of Katherine is the way she holds her breath at night and the way I roll her over so she'll exhale.

My gut bloats and swells, alive with lead weight and gas. The skin on my face stretches tighter and tighter, my cheeks tingle with fire. I swallow hard; some viscous mucus slides down my throat and for a moment I lay back on the ground dizzy with a thousand questions ripping through my brain:

What happens next?

Why didn't I finish grouting the bathroom?

Will it hurt?

I wish I'd told him I loved him.

Can I go....

"Can I go back?" I ask sitting up with a damp snort, another slimy gulp, that 'tch-ah' noise you make when breathing out through a wet smile.

I expect him to ask "why?" and I have a thousand reasons ready to pummel him with but instead he drops the cigarette on the pavement, twists one of his boots with a griddle crunch, licks the taste of the filter from his lips and says, "Sure." Just like that. My cheeks begin to dry with the touch of soft, cold air before white light stings my eyes and somewhere the old man's voice says that I'm going to be all right. Another voice I don't recognise tells me to stay awake and that they're cutting me out and that I should stay awake but I can't anymore. In the dark of my eyelids sparks dance, metal shrieks and a damp trickle tickles down the side of my face. My head feels fat and tight as it pounds and pounds and pounds.

Like a pendulum, my head hangs limp and long and, for a moment, I feel peaceful…

I drove along the road by the park the other day. I wasn't sure what I was expecting, or what I was hoping to find, but there weren't any flowers on the ground by the sign, just the bare grass verge and the pavement and the oak trees.

I couldn't bring myself to tell anyone about the strange old man. Everything feels so delicate since I met him. I found myself not only afraid to speak but equally wary of silence as if everything might just fade away like a curl of smoke.

Stood by the side of the road a part of me felt misplaced knowing he'd taken my white flowers back. Another part can't stop thinking about the cat who should have looked both ways. I have no idea why.

About the author:
Daniel (@D_Dowsing) is a writer and game narrative designer. He writes weird fiction in the form of short stories, comics and computer games. He is the co-creator of online graphic novel *The Wolf* (www.thewolfonline.net) and his short comic story *I Remember You* is being published by GreyHaven Comics. His gaming credits include: *Recovery Search & Rescue Simulator* and *Primal Rumble*. Maybe one day he'll be writing for Doctor Who.

The Green of His Eyes

Sarah Bakewell

Her right foot started tapping like it always did when she was nervous. She peered out of the steamy bus window and took in the late autumn evening, shifting uncomfortably in her seat. The sun had almost fully retreated behind the tall buildings, leaving the sky a hazy violet with an inky darkness slowly bleeding through the air. There were fewer street lights now. By the time the bus reached her stop, the sky had turned a deep navy blue.

Alex set off along the pavement, her shadow dragging itself reluctantly behind her. Her heartbeat quickened with every step. *Keep going,* she told herself. *You have to do this for her; you have to make her proud.*

She stopped in front of the boarded-up working men's club. This was it – the place she'd approached countless times in the last few weeks, trying to find out if the rumours were true. Trying to catch a glimpse of him – to make sure. Trying. The night air shuddered through her lungs. Wishing she'd told someone where she was going, she strutted round to the side door of the abandoned building. She remembered to ruffle her hair in the direction of the CCTV camera she already knew was there.

Raising her head and cocking it to one side, she lifted a fist, swallowed, and, for the first time, she knocked. Footsteps. She transferred her weight across to her right leg and placed her trembling hand on her hip, attempting to look confident, mirroring the movements of a girl she'd seen enter the club last week. With a creak, the door pulled into the building to reveal a slice of the dusty, dimly-lit room. Whoever opened it stayed behind the door.

They didn't say a word. She stepped into the building, jumping not at the thud of the door closing, but at the clunk of the heavy bolt thudding home.

"Through there," a deep voice growled from behind her. She went to stride forwards, but her feet only managed a small, slow shuffle. The doorman grew impatient and pressed his large palm into the small of her back, pushing her through large, open double doors, and into what would have once been a meeting room. The furniture had been pushed to the sides and covered in large white cloths. The doorman gave her a final small shove and left quietly, thankfully leaving the doors open. A group of men stood under one of the bare light bulbs, apparently deep in hushed discussion.

It was him – Alex recognised him instantly. He looked exactly as he did when she was six, aside from a few added wrinkles and strands of grey in his hair. Alex remembered very little of her childhood, but she recalled with absolute clarity the weeks leading up to when she last saw him, ten years ago.

"When's Daddy coming home?" It was the second evening he'd not been there. He'd often worked late, so her dad missing her bedtime the night before wasn't unusual. He usually left very early for work too, so his empty seat at the breakfast table the following morning hadn't concerned her. This time was longer. It was different. Her mum was different. When she asked, her mum just pulled her into a lavender-scented hug and pressed her lips on her daughter's head.

"He's… been taken from us."

"Has he gone on another work holiday?"

She looked sadly at her daughter. "No, sweetheart."

"But he's coming back soon, right?"

There were never any explanations or answers. Instead, her mum packed a bag of Alex's clothes and Alex spent a week with her grandparents while her mum 'dealt with some things' at home. She didn't ask much; she got a week off school, who was she to complain? Her grandparents kept her entertained with walking their dogs and letting her help bake cakes; she often forgot why she was there. When her mum brought her home a week later, Alex realised all of her dad's stuff had gone. She asked why and where her daddy was again, but her mum didn't answer. She simply hugged her daughter.

There seemed to be an increasing number of visitors, none of whom were ever invited in. They'd got a doorbell a few weeks before; her mum had always said that knocks were often unheard and it gave the postman an excuse to steal their parcels. She let Alex pick the tune she liked best and they'd installed a doorbell that could be heard everywhere in their house – their neighbours frequently complained that they could hear it too. They stopped complaining after her dad had gone, which Alex found odd considering how much it was ringing now. Her mum would go to the door, shutting Alex in the front room with her after-school cartoons, and would come back a few minutes later by herself. Alex never saw who was coming round; her mum had taken to not opening the curtains. Sometimes when her mum came back, she'd be clutching flowers and what looked like unopened birthday cards.

"Who was at the door, Mummy? Was it Daddy? Has he come back?"

"No, sweetheart… It was nobody."

"What're they?" She'd point to the flowers and cards.

"Nothing."

Her mum always took any flowers and cards straight through the house and to the bins by the back door. Alex didn't ask any more about them. It wasn't either of their birthdays, after all.

She'd had a day off school in the run up to Christmas; her mum said it was for something very important. Instead of donning her usual blue jumper, black pleated skirt, and white knee-length socks, her mum had picked out a rather dull-looking black dress for Alex to wear. Her mum, once again, didn't respond to Alex's questions about where they were going and why was she still crying, but instead kissed her daughter on the head and asked her to put the dress on. She remembered it being itchy.

In the car, Alex hadn't been paying attention to where they were going. It was only when her Disney CD stopped playing that she'd looked out of the window. They were in a relatively small car park with a ticket machine to the left of where her mum had parked. She watched her mum pressing the buttons and feeding it the coins; Alex now noticed that her mum was wearing black too.

They arrived in the marble entrance of the court, her mother grasping her small hand firmly. Alex clung to her mother when they got there; people were looking at them. She thought it was because her dress looked stupid. Her mum led her down the corridor to a quieter area and a row of chairs; Alex climbed onto the chair furthest from the crowds.

"Wait here a minute, sweetheart," her mum whispered to her as she went to shoo away a man with a camera and notepad, leaving Alex alone on her chair.

Alex stared silently at her shiny black shoes that didn't reach the floor, and began swinging them back and forth in frustration. She was aware of the people looking down the corridor at her and whispering. She stared hard at the reflective floor, gripping the chair with all her might, until her mum's heels came into view, closely followed by her

174

bent legs, before a finger glided slowly into sight and gently tilted her chin up.

"Alex, I know this is strange..." her mum began, crouched in front of her.

"They think my dress is stupid."

"Sweetheart, they don't. You look lovely."

Alex would not look at her mother. Her eyes were flicking about everywhere else – anywhere else. She looked at the golden chandeliers, the white-patterned ceiling, the tall gleaming windows. She'd been listening to the thudding echoes of footsteps up and down the corridor and the excited mutterings around them. She caught the scent of her mother's lavender perfume as she furiously breathed in with clamped lips.

"Alex... It's, it's really important that you're... That we're here." The familiar, confident voice of her mother had vanished. Instead, her mum spoke in a whisper. A clumsy whisper. Alex looked up and into her mother's eyes and saw a shimmer of liquid glazed across them. She leapt out of her seat and threw her arms around her mum's neck, clasping her clammy hands together when they met.

"Why are you crying?" she whispered into her mum's ear through the strands of blonde hair that had come loose from their clip.

"I'm not darling..." She unfastened her daughter and drew back before placing her hands firmly on Alex's shoulders. "Do you know why we're here?" Alex shook her head. Her mum took a large, visible breath. "We're here to start our lives again, just you and me. Very soon, you'll have to be a very brave girl and see the man that ruined..." She caught herself. "... That *changed* our lives. The man who took your father away from us."

Alex continued to look at her mother. She blinked slowly.

175

"Daddy's not coming back, is he?"

"... You don't have a daddy anymore, sweetheart. I'm so sorry." There was a sudden flurry of people, of noise, of flashes from the front doors of the court. Alex's mum picked up her daughter and carried her back to the crowds gathered around the entrance. She rested her daughter on her hip, just so Alex's head bobbed up above the herd of frenzied people. She looked down at the scalps of people shaking their fists and shouting, some of whom were waving large signs. She tried to hold on to her mother, to get down.

"You stay there, sweetheart, my brave girl," her mum shouted to her over the chaos, anger threaded in her voice. Her mum hitched Alex a little higher up on her side. "You look at him when he comes in!" she was yelling now. "He ruined your life!"

There were jeers from the crowds. Someone bumped into Alex's mum, making her and Alex sway. Alex felt her mother's grip tighten. Large men in suits were holding back the crowds as police officers escorted a man inside.

Although flustered and ambushed, Alex saw his eyes lock on hers above the crowd. He stared directly back at her. He looked like... She called out, but her words were lost amongst the crowd. He didn't hear her – she couldn't hear herself. He was almost level with her now. She noticed the shape of his ears, the green of his eyes, the flick at the end of his nose. She tried to yell louder, desperate for him to hear her, wanting him to say something – for it all to stop. He stared back, but only for a second as he was rushed through the angry mobs and swept away by the police, but there was no mistaking it. He'd seen her.

He hadn't seen her now, but she'd definitely seen him. There he was, in the grotty boarded-up club with a bunch

176

of, by the look of it, other criminals. He hadn't noticed her being pushed in. None of them had. She stood perfectly still, burning her eyes into the profile of the man who ruined her and her mother's lives. Oh yes. She'd definitely seen him now.

She hadn't learnt the true facts about the murder until years later. She'd found out from someone else, someone in her tutor group at secondary school. It was exciting gossip to her peers, discussed openly with no veils of condolence or consideration of feelings. She'd stormed home and demanded to know why nobody had ever told her how she really lost her dad. Her mother said she'd been waiting until she was old enough to understand – that she hadn't thought it would have come out like that.

The pair had sat and shouted and cried and got up again and screamed and apologised and cried some more before finally, together, they slumped onto the sofa and held each other. It wasn't just Alex who'd lost her father; it was also her struggling mum who'd lost her husband.

The man standing in front of her now was the reason she'd grown up without a father, and why her mother had battled to be the single parent, trying to raise her daughter away from the scandal. Alex remembered why she was there. She adopted the confident stance she'd practised in her room – hand on hip, shoulders back, legs slightly apart – and she coughed.

One or two looked round and whistled. She kept her eyes firmly on him as he flicked his dark hair from his face. He was in deep conversation with one of the others who hadn't turned.

"And who might you be, little lady?" A large, greasy man broke from the group and took a few slow steps towards her. She hadn't prepared for this. This wasn't part of the plan. The dark-haired man was supposed to notice her.

"Jade," she invented, pulling herself together and shifting her slight weight from one leg to the other. "But you can call me whatever you want."

"Can I, indeed?" he chuckled, glancing back at the seedy men behind him, doing something Alex couldn't see, blocked by his frame. It resulted in roaring laughter from the men that were paying attention.

"Give it to her, Johnny!"

Johnny turned round, his lips stretched up one side of his face. He took another step closer. Alex panicked and took half a step back.

She regretted it instantly.

"Ooh, shy now are we? That's all right, we'll take good care of you…" Johnny licked his lips. Behind him, she saw, the men that were laughing had nudged the dark-haired man and his acquaintance out of conversation, and he'd looked up at last, squinting.

His eyes bulged in recognition. She stared back and raised her chin, aiming to appear confident, while she bit the inside of her lip. Johnny, she realised, had crept up on her while she was staring at the dark-haired man behind him.

"Look at me!" Johnny went to grab Alex's hair.

"GET OFF HER!" It was him. The dark-haired man. The one she wanted, pushing through the crowd towards them.

Johnny let his bulky arm fall and took a step back, turning to address the interruption.

"All right, Charlie boy, what's gotten into you? She's no different than that piece the other week. I don't recall you objecting then."

178

"I want her," he said, staring directly into Alex's eyes now that he'd reached Johnny's side. "She's mine."

These statements resulted in more whistles from the pack, and chuckles from Johnny, who went to put his arm around Alex. "Selfish bastard, isn't he love?" His hand dropped to her lower back, and then a little lower. "Tell you what, you can go first," he bellowed to the others, giving Alex a squeeze, "and then you can pass her round." Laughter.

"Fine," he barked, storming up to the pair and grabbing Alex by the arm, pulling her free. She shook her arm out of his grasp angrily and led herself back through the double doors and into the entrance room. It was empty now. The doorman had either gone, or was waiting in the shadows; Alex didn't know – she didn't care. She stormed on, the dark-haired man closely behind her, and they ended up back out in the street. She spun round to face him. She'd never imagined she'd get this opportunity, the chance to see him again and confront him.

"What the fuck are you doing here?" he hissed, slamming the door shut behind him.

"Could ask you the same thing, Dad."

He stepped back and forth and to the side, furiously tugging at his dark hair. "Look at the fucking state of you."

"Don't start playing the role of a doting father. Besides, you think they'd have let me into your seedy little club wearing a jumper and jeans?"

His eyes widened. "You knew I was here?"

"Of course I did! I'm not a slapper. I could hardly knock on the door and say 'Excuse me but I'd like a little chat with my estranged twat of a father' could I?" She paused, shocked at the words her anger produced.

"Alex…"

"No. I don't want to hear it. I'm not here for excuses or fake apologies or anything like that." She was breathing heavily now, realising how furious she was at him. "I've come here to tell you to your *face*," – she almost spat the word at him – "that I'm disgusted you're my father. I hate you. I actually hate you."

She stopped and stepped back, shaking furiously, suddenly having no idea what to do; the speech she'd practised for weeks, ever since she'd seen the headlines confirming his release, had vanished. He looked almost harmless. She looked in his eyes. His sad eyes.

No, she instructed herself, clenching her fists, *don't you dare feel sorry for him. He's a murderer. He took a life and left you and your mother to face the consequences; the hate mail, the bullying. It's all his fault.*

"Your mother was having an affair," he said bluntly. All the anger had gone from his voice.

She snapped out of her thoughts and scrunched up her face in confusion. "What?"

"She said you weren't mine."

She noticed the shape of his ears, like hers, and the green of his eyes, like hers. The flick at the end of his nose. Like hers.

"I don't believe you."

"Why would you? I don't expect you to. It's not true…I mean, the affair was, but you're mine."

"Why would she make stuff up? And… Just… Stop trying to justify what you did!"

"I'm not, I'm just trying to explain. Your mother hated me. She wanted to hurt me. It went down as manslaughter – we were both drunk. He came up to me… I had no idea of any affair. He started prodding me, goading me. Started saying my little girl was his little girl…" He trailed off. "I accept responsibility for my actions, Alex, and I've done my time. But don't you dare think I'm the sole reason for any of this. See – look at your face! That spiteful bitch never told you."

She furrowed her brows and closed her mouth; she realised it had been hanging open throughout his speech.

"You're lying."

"Ask her."

She couldn't speak, and he said nothing more. She clawed her hands through her hair then threw her arms back by her sides, exasperated.

"I've nothing to say to you," she asserted, drawing herself up. He opened his mouth to speak, but a series of thuds from the club made the pair jump.

"Charlie boy! What's taking so long? You're usually the first to finish! Come on, man, we're *starving* in here!"

Alex scrunched her face up in disgust and turned away. Her dad caught her by the arm and pulled her back, fumbling in his pocket with his free hand.

"You listen to me. Take this," he pushed a wad of notes into her sweaty palm, "and get the fuck out of here. Go up by that bus stop, turn left down there, and onto the main road. There's a taxi rank. Go home."

"I'm not taking your…"

"You are. Go. Don't come back here." He gave her hand another push and let go. "I'll deal with them." She didn't move. Bangs and jeers echoed from the club. "Alex, go."

She turned and ran, past the bus stop, left, and to the main road. Her feet pounded the ground. She clambered into the first taxi, struggling to catch her breath as she said her address. The taxi started up and swung back around, heading slowly down the narrow alley she'd just run up.

181

They passed the club. Her dad was still outside. Waiting. She'd seen him. And through the misty glass that separated them, she knew that his green eyes had seen her.

About the author:
Sarah Bakewell works in publishing by day but writes dark short fiction by night. Her work has previously been published by Jessica Kingsley Publishers, Chapeltown, and Dying Matters, with stories appearing in *Best of CaféLit 2012* and *Darker Times Anthology: Volume Two*. Although currently situated in London with her fiancé Andy, she will always be a Northerner at heart.

The Patient

Glynis Scrivens

Death knocked on the door.

The nurse didn't notice him. She was busy inspecting the feeding tube and oxygen mask of her patient. These hours were crucial.

Lying on the bed, eyes closed, Sheila was only too well aware of his presence. She'd met him once before, years ago, during a very difficult labour. She knew he'd wait stubbornly, but she could be stubborn as well. She hoped that would be enough. It would be cruel for Death to take her now, just as she'd become a grandmother. And she knew James would never manage on his own.

She was intermittently aware of the warm pressure of James's hand. If only she could signal to him that she was still here, fighting on, in her fragile frame.

She knew she looked fragile. She'd seen herself just a few moments ago, before Death knocked. It'd been like a waking dream, floating above her body. How pale her face had looked. And she was shocked to see how many machines seemed to be linked up to her body, keeping it from Death's clutches. No wonder James looked so worried.

"I'm going to be fine, darling," she wanted to say. But she knew that was far from the truth.

She'd heard the private conversation between the doctor and the nurse, out of James's hearing. It hadn't been very hard to read between the lines.

"It's touch and go," he'd said. "We'll have to see if she responds to these new antibiotics."

The nurse nodded. "Visiting hours are over. What should I say to her husband?"

"Just let him stay here. It might give her extra strength. They seem a very devoted couple." He'd paused. "And if she doesn't respond, it'll all be very quick. We may not be able to reach him in time."

Something in Sheila's soul had relaxed at those words, sobering as they were. She needed James here. And if she must go with Death, she'd want him here to say goodbye.

The strange thing was, she didn't even know what had gone wrong in her body. She'd been in the kitchen, getting out the ingredients for pastry. She wanted to bake an apple pie to take over to her daughter that afternoon. It'd happened in a moment. A wave of dread and nausea as she fell to the floor. She had no recollection of the ambulance arriving or of being brought here to the intensive care unit. She'd evidently had an operation. In her more lucid moments she was aware of an acute pain in her side, and she'd seen the dressings earlier.

And she was aware, perhaps more so than ever before, of how deeply she loved James. They'd been married for nearly forty years now. It'd been love at first sight, that day he'd come to the optometrist's and she'd helped him choose a pair of frames.

She wanted to share this special memory with him. And to ask him what had happened to her. It was hard being unable to communicate at such an important time.

If she had the energy, she'd smile. A memory had been stirred and it made her want to laugh. To share the thought.

As a young child, she'd often played doctors and nurses with her sister. They'd giggle as they pretended to suffer from bizarre embarrassing maladies. Often they'd joke about being two souls in heaven, comparing notes about how they'd died. "It started with my hands turning purple," one of them would say. "Then my body turned to ice." It became a competition to invent the worst scenario. Falling off a mountain, while blindfolded. Drowning in a puddle. Being struck by the only bolt of lightning during a storm, while hiding naked under a big tree. Eating red berries then discovering they were poisonous.

Never in all their games had they thought of this. The "I don't know what I died of" scenario.

Somehow it was important to let her sister know they'd missed the funniest one.

Her reverie was interrupted.

"Did you see that?" she heard James say to the nurse. She felt him press her hand as he brought it to his lips. "I thought I saw her eyelids flicker."

She felt the closer presence of the nurse, checking her pulse. Heard the reassuring but non-committal comments of the nurse. "It'll be a few hours yet before we know whether she's turned the corner." "It's a promising development, but we can't get our hopes up yet." And so on.

There was another knock on the door. *Who could have the nerve to stand there, beside Death?* she thought.

Or had he left to seek another soul? Was it someone else's turn to become the object of his vigil?

No, he was still there. Sheila could sense the grey chill of his presence.

But there was light, warmth, there as well.

And she heard the soft gurgling noises of a baby. Little Rose. Sheila's heart melted as she dimly sensed the soft sweet warmth as her granddaughter's cheek was placed on her own. A gossamer caress, as though an angel had touched her with a feather. Sheila's heart lightened. She felt her daughter's kiss. "Hang in there, Mum," she whispered.

She drifted off into a zone of light, as sensations gave

way to unconsciousness. Dim voices. Nothingness. The warmth of James's hand. Light.

Some time later she was aware that she was in pain. Her right side ached, stung, grumbled. Yet she felt a gentle strength returning.

She could hear the unmistakeable steady regular breathing of James sleeping. He must've spent the night here, slumped over the end of the bed where she'd seen him earlier.

As she tried to open her eyes, she noticed a grey form in the doorway. A gentle smile of understanding on his face, Death faded away. She was spared. Given more precious time to enjoy the company of her loved ones. Sheila pressed James's hand as she opened her eyes. She felt blessed to be alive.

About the author:
Glynis Scrivens writes short stories, and has been published in Australia, UK, Ireland, South Africa, US and Scandinavia. She writes for *Writers' Forum* (UK). She has had articles in *Pets*, *Steam Railway*, *Ireland's Own*, *The New Writer* and *Writing* magazine. Her work has appeared in seven anthologies. She lives in Brisbane with her family and a menagerie of hens, ducks, dogs, lorikeets, and a cat called Myrtle.

The Tramp

Anne Wilson

This year is called nineteen hundred and fifty, and two things have happened; I was seven and, as well, I had my photograph taken at school. Mummy bought four, one for our mantelpiece, one for Nana and Grampy, one for Grandma and Grandad, and a spare one.

There's a gap in my front teeth, I've got things Mummy says are freckles; what are they? Why are they there? I don't like my hair plaited. For special occasions, Mummy makes loops with my plaits and ties them behind my ears with ribbons. I hate that, it feels silly.

Daddy said I looked very grown up but I don't want to look grown up because it's nearly Christmas and grown-ups don't get very many presents off Father Christmas. If I look *very* grown up I might not get *any*. I'm trying not to look grown up because I think he can see me because Mummy says he always knows if I've been good. How does he know?

Christmas is nearly here and I feel really worried that Father Christmas might not come.

On a Saturday I go with Mummy, to the market for the Big Shop. We go every week, but one week I had to stay with Nana because Mummy had some secret shopping to do but I don't know why she wouldn't take me because I wouldn't tell anyone.

On the way to market Mummy always gives a whole packet of cigarettes to a funny-looking man called The Tramp. Sometimes he's called The Tramp and sometimes Mummy calls him The Poor Soul when Daddy asks if she gave him the cigarettes. Cigarettes and matches are very dangerous and I'm not allowed to touch them, but I know where they are; they're on the mantelpiece behind the clock.

The cigarettes make The Tramp smile and nod his head; he always nods his head a lot but I don't know what he says because of his beard. I can't remember seeing him smoking but I think it would be too difficult with his crutch because he has to keep it under his arm all the time. Sometimes when he talks, he coughs, then he has to get his handkerchief out of his pocket and that's all a bit difficult.

The Tramp stands on a step, in a very high doorway in front of a very big, heavy door at the back of where the Co-Op Savings Bank is. He looks funny, dressed in old grey clothes, with his big, bushy beard and he has a crutch with lots of material wrapped round it like bandages. You'd think the bandages would be on him, not the crutch. They always look as if they need washing. I don't know if you iron bandages.

He wears a row of medals pinned to his jacket, which makes him look dressed up but his clothes are dirty. I think he must spill his dinner a bit, down his jacket, and if he's dressed up, why doesn't he wear his best shoes instead of his slippers? He's got a big scarf as well and some raggy gloves with no fingers on the ends. I think he smells funny and his beard needs combing; it's going a bit yellow but I don't know why. I never say anything to him, but I think he smiles at me a bit.

He must live inside the door, not coming all the way out on Saturdays because the street is so busy and his crutch is big under his arm and it makes him lean over. He keeps the door always closed because what's inside must be secret.

I think of the hallway on the other side of his great door and the grand rooms that must lead off it. There must be high ceilings and staircases and thick red carpets. I can see lots of lights; like in the ballroom when Cinderella danced with the Handsome Prince. I always wonder why people give The Tramp things when he lives in such a big important-looking house.

Saturday shopping always ends with a visit to Burtons Café on the corner of Lord Street, where the waitresses wear white aprons and caps. Mummy and I sit upstairs beside a front window so I can watch the trams go past. Mummy sits opposite to me. She keeps her packet of cigarettes and her gold cigarette lighter on the table. She has a home perm on her hair and wears red lipstick. She wears a hat with a brown bird's feather in it and the coat she always wears. She has a coat called Beaver Lamb, but she doesn't wear that on Saturdays.

I always have a crumbly pastry with cream and jam. Mummy always has a drink of tea and a meringue. Then I have to sit still while she has a cigarette. I like to watch the smoke from cigarettes to see what it will do. It always makes a different pattern in the air but I don't like the way it smells.

I sometimes think about The Tramp. Last Saturday he wasn't on his step. I asked Mummy where he was but she said she didn't know. Sometimes I think grown-ups *do* know things but they don't want to tell you because they don't want *you* to know, but I don't know why.

I've worked out The Tramp's secret and it's something I know and the grown-ups don't. They can't see that he's Father Christmas in disguise. No-one else in the whole world has a beard like that and the big house must be where he stores the presents. Perhaps there's even room for the elves and the reindeer. The money he collects in his tin is to pay for the presents. I know someone has to pay for them because Mummy keeps telling me. The old clothes are a good disguise and so is the crutch. When The Tramp smiles at me I think he knows that I know who he is. It's our secret and I'll never tell.

When Mummy finishes her cigarette it's time to go home. She always puts some money under her teacup and saucer and brushes the cigarette ash off the tablecloth. It leaves grey marks. I always look back to see if someone finds the money. If I see them, they never look surprised or pleased; just put it in the pocket in their apron.

Last Saturday when we got home Mummy put away the shopping and Daddy came home for tea. After tea, the Chronicle was on the table. There was a picture of The Tramp, The Poor Soul, with his Father Christmas beard. Next to the picture was a war picture of a soldier wearing his uniform. The soldier looked a bit like The Tramp but I think he was younger and he hadn't got a beard.

I couldn't read the name under the picture of The Tramp but the number was easy; it was forty-two. If that's his age they must have got it wrong because Daddy is forty-two and he doesn't look old like The Tramp. I think you have to be very old to have a great big beard.

Mummy was clearing the table.

"Look," I said, "it's The Tramp. Why is he in the paper? Is he famous?"

"He died." Mummy said and folded the paper and put it on the shelf. She had to do the washing up.

I sat at the table with my book.

Why does he want people to think he's dead? Is he dead? I wonder where his medals are and if someone else will wear them. What about his grand house with the big door and the high ceilings and thick carpets; who will live there now?

I wondered if he's still inside and has a lot of secret work to do behind his big door, getting ready for Christmas.

That would be why he's not there. He must have collected enough money to pay for the presents and now he has to wrap them all up. I know that the elves help him, but it's still a very big job.

I went into the kitchen and asked Mummy, "could we help The Tramp?"

Mummy was washing up; she gave me a funny look. "I told you; I'm sorry, he's dead. It's too late to help him. It's very sad. He's like your rabbit, Fluffy, he won't come back. You won't see him again? Do you understand?"

She used her kind voice, so I nodded my head and went back to my book.

Today is Saturday; it's Christmas Eve and I looked at The Tramp's doorway but it was empty again. I wanted to knock on the big closed door but Mummy wouldn't let me; she says I have to forget about him. She says she thinks he got too cold.

I don't think Mummy understands.

I've opened the last picture on my advent calendar; I'm really worried about if I get any presents tonight.

About the author:
Anne grew up on the west coast of Britain, also living on the Balearic island of Mallorca. She was employed to deliver the Government initiative of Additional Literacy Support in schools while gaining a BA in linguistics and creative writing. Her short fiction appears in a number of anthologies and her first novel *Here Be Dragons: A Tale of Mortals, Myths and Mystery* is available in print and e-format.

www.authoranne.co.uk

Index of Authors

Other Publications by Bridge House

Something Hidden

edited by Debz Hobbs-Wyatt and Gill James

There is something hidden, something darker and something challenging behind that placid veneer of calmness we so often see in everyday life. We asked for something a little darker for our latest short story competition. The entrants certainly supplied that. In this anthology we've collected the strongest. Each of the stories makes you think.

"Loved this story (*Home*) in particular as it resonated with me but all of the stories were enjoyable and well weitten." (*Amazon*)

Order from www.bridgehousepublishing.co.uk

Paperback: ISBN 978-1-907335-31-0
eBook: ISBN 978-1-907335-33-4

Otherwhere and Elsewhen

Tales of alternative realities

edited by Gill James

Are we alone? Surely not. Do other realities exist? They must do mustn't they? This can't be it, can it?

If you weren't convinced before, you certainly will be after you've read this collection of stories that take place in another time and another space, light years from here. Come read and discover what happened otherwhere and elsewhen.

"If you love Si-FI then you should definitely get this. The Authors have great imaginations and have created some fantastic worlds."
(*Amazon*)

Order from www.bridgehousepublishing.co.uk

Paperback: ISBN 978-1-907335-23-5
eBook: ISBN 978-1-907335-28-0